MADE FOR SIN

CASS KINCAID

Published in the United States of America by EverLust Books an imprint of Harbor Lane Books, LLC.

www.everlustbooks.com

PROLOGUE
ASHTON

TWELVE YEARS AGO...

AT ONE POINT IN TIME, I probably would have thought that being turned down by Layla Miller when I asked her to prom was the biggest blow to my ego I'd ever experienced. It sucked when it happened, and I still can't figure out where I went wrong. I mean, she's the captain of the cheerleading squad, and I'm the quarterback for our school's football team. We're supposed to go together like—

Whatever, that's beside the point now. Because the only thing worse than getting rejected by Layla, is having to celebrate my eighteenth goddamn birthday alongside my best friend's little sister.

I don't begrudge the girl having a party. Hell, she can take all her little teeny bopper friends and go catch a sugar high at some Hannah Montana concert, if that's what they want to do.

And that's what they *should* want to do.

Which is exactly why I'm mortified and disgusted by the fact that my parents think it's just fucking dandy to shove our families together and have an outdoor dinner and celebration in our backyard, celebrating my eighteenth birthday…and Sadie's twelfth.

Sadie's brother, Gerard—or Gunner, as he's always been called—is my best friend, and he has been since I can remember. We've lived beside each other our entire lives, and our parents are best friends with each other, too. It's sickeningly insane, really, just how interconnected and entwined our families are.

But having a joint birthday party with a godforsaken twelve-year-old? That's a new low, even for our parents.

And Sadie's not even the shy, quiet preteen that might have enough grace to eat her fucking birthday cake and leave me alone. No, Sadie Mitchell is boisterous, animated, and annoying as hell.

"It's just a backyard BBQ with the Mitchells and a few friends, Ashton. You'll survive." My mother shoots me a glare, and for once it's not because of the ripped holes in my jeans or the curse words coming from my mouth.

"Explain to me again why I have to be there for cake and ice cream with the Mitchells, Mom, because I don't get it. You want to celebrate Sadie's birthday, go right ahead. But, she's twelve. I can think of better things to do with my time." I pull my denim jacket from the back of the kitchen chair, shrugging it on. I don't know where I'm planning to go, but there's got to be somewhere better than here, with an impending joint birthday party with a kid.

"Oh, stop. It'll be fun. You know that Rick and Anna enjoy the fact that you and Sadie have the same birthday, almost as much as your father and I do. It's like fate brought us together," she rambles on.

I can't hold back, and I roll my eyes dramatically. "We're not Mitchells, Mom. And they're not Butlers. We're two separate families, in case you and Dad haven't noticed."

I watch as Mom puts the finishing touches on the cake she's working meticulously on, never once turning her attention away from it to look at me. I also notice that the cake has white and purple icing. Girl colors.

They can call it whatever they want, but the backyard party they're tossing me into is for Sadie, the Mitchells' daughter.

The daughter my Mom and Dad always wanted, but never got. Instead, they're stuck with me, and they make no efforts to hide their disappointment in that fact.

"We're practically family," she halfheartedly argues back.

"We share a lot line with them, Mom. Not blood. Not last names. They're neighbors. We can do things without the Mitchells every now and then, you know."

Her lips pull tighter then, and her gaze flickers to me for a split second. "That's enough, Ashton. I mean it. You and Gunner have been inseparable basically since birth, so I really don't know where—"

"Gunner and I are the same age!"

"And Gunner will be at the birthday party at five o'clock," Mom says briskly. "And so will you, so you'll have each other to keep company, if you can't bring yourself to give Sadie a few moments of your time on her special day."

It's on the tip of my tongue to remind her that it's my day, too. It's *my* goddamn birthday, and all I want to do is spend it with someone other than a goddamn twelve-year-old girl. But there's no use. Mom isn't listening now, just like she hasn't listened for the last eighteen years I've been alive.

The Mitchells and the Butlers will always be one and the same, as far as she's concerned. And Gunner—yeah, he's been my best friend since before we could walk, but I understand that we aren't brothers.

Like brothers, sure. But not from the same family.

And I sure as hell am not Sadie Mitchell's brother, either. The last thing I want to be is any closer to that annoying little girl than I have to be.

———

"I thought eighteenth birthdays were supposed to be full of stolen liquor and chicks in the backseat of our cars?" Gunner stares straight ahead, his elbows leaning against the back of the top of the picnic table, legs sprawled out in front of him. "How the fuck did we get lucky enough to be here, with our parents, and Sadie, eating hamburgers and chocolate cake?"

His summation does little to help my mood out. "Your guess is as good as mine." I sit beside him, drinking Pepsi from the can in my hands. We both have done everything we could for the past hour to avoid hanging out with our parents or their friends. "You can thank your sister for this."

That comment earns me a cocked eyebrow from him. "Seriously? You can't blame her. It's not like she purposely was born on your birthday to spite you. It's their fault." Gunner juts his chin out toward the group of adults on the patio. "Our parents have gone all fucking Brady Bunch on us. One big happy family, and all that."

"They can't tell where your family stops, and mine begins." I narrow my eyes. "It's bullshit."

"Easy, killer." Gunner shifts, but by now he should've realized how impossible it is to get comfortable on a picnic table. "If it's any consolation, my eighteenth is in two months. We'll do it up right, then."

I give him a sideways glance, the thought of it making the corners of my mouth turn up. "Now, we're talking. Can you get the keys to your dad's Camaro?"

"Can you talk Ashley and Madison from our history class into joyriding with us?"

"The twins in the back row?" I didn't even know he'd been interested in them. But, hell, who wasn't? "Shit, that'd be some birthday present, Gunner."

"Think you can sweet talk 'em?" He grins, nudging me.

"There's two. Might be able to salvage some of *your* birthday, too."

"Damn." I run my hand through my shaggy chestnut hair, wincing slightly as I think about the work I'd have cut out for me to pull off such a feat. "Which one do you want?"

"Madison," Gunner replies without hesitation. "That chick's been eye-fucking me for weeks."

I let out a low whistle. "Can't say I'm complaining if I can do Ashley."

"That means you'll do whatever the fuck it is you do, and charm them into partying with us?"

I swore after Layla turned me down that I'd lay low. I know damn well my reputation got in the way of that deal—it was no secret that I could talk the panties off pretty much any girl in our grade. "Ah, hell, why not? I like a challenge."

Gunner shakes his head, chuckling. "You really are a manwhore, aren't you?"

"You aren't much better, you realize that, right?" I smile, my first real smile since this stupid party got underway. "You'll screw any—"

I feel something hit the back of my neck before I hear the hissing sound that accompanies it. Stumbling away from the table, I clamp my hand down on my neck, feeling something wet. "What the—"

All at once, I realize that the substance is a bright shade of blue, that it's still coming at me, covering my shoulders, back, and head...and that there's a loud wave of high-pitched shrieks assaulting my ears.

I turn around, holding my jacket up as best as I can to shield myself, but it's no use. "Come on!" I bellow, pissed off at the gang of young girls. "Fucking silly string? That's enough!"

But the shrill laughter continues.

Every ounce of anger I feel about this party, this stupid family dynamic, and this *day* erupts inside me. Lowering my jacket and seeing Sadie there, with her finger pressed down on the silly string canister, only makes my blood reach its boiling point.

"Happy birthday, Ashton!" she screams, her laughter so loud and obnoxious that there are stray tears on her cheeks. The young girl weaves one way, then the next, trying to keep far enough away from me so that I won't take the aerosol can from her, but never once lets up on the steady stream of string that continues to propel toward me.

"You think this is fucking funny?"

"Ash—"

I can hear Gunner trying to calm me down. Our parents are probably yelling a blue streak, too, because I've just cursed at their fucking beloved Sadie, but I can't hear them over my pounding pulse.

In one fell swoop, I dive for the canister in her hand. I grab Sadie by the wrist with one hand, and tear the can from her fingers with the other.

Her laughter stops immediately. "Hey!"

I let her go, turn, and pitch the canister high into the air, into the heavily treed area behind our house. "I told you to fucking stop!"

Sadie stands there, wide-eyed, her handful of friends tucked in close behind her, not saying a word. Her voice comes out no louder than a whisper. "I just—"

"You just what? Wanted to be a pain in the ass?" The words come out of me in a tsunami of pent-up rage, fed up with having to put up with this ridiculous charade any longer. "Because you're succeeding. That's all you are...a pain in my goddamn ass!"

Sadie's bottom lip quivers, and any decent man probably would have left it at that. But I can't seem to stop myself.

"You're just a fucking kid! Go play with your Barbie dolls, or whatever the hell you irritating little girls do!" I yell.

"Ashton! Cool it!" Gunner barks.

But the damage has been done. A thin line of tears streak Sadie's face. Despite her small stature and her thin frame, she stays standing there, taking each verbal blow as it comes. "But…it's our birthday. I thought we were friends—"

"Friends?" I choke out the word like it tastes bad, running my hand through my hair, still tangled with blue string. "We're not friends. Or family, for that matter, but you'd never fucking know it with this crap still going on every year." I glare around me, at everyone who's now stopped talking, stopped breathing, mortified by my outburst. "And *our* birthday? Christ, keep it, Sadie. I'm through sharing it. You can fucking have it."

I know I've crossed a line, and I damn well know I'm an asshole for taking it out on a kid, but that doesn't stop me from turning away from that little girl's tear-streaked face and storming past everyone on the patio.

No one says a word. Which is good, because by the time I hit the pavement of the driveway, I'm not sure there's anything anyone could say that would make me feel any worse than I already do.

CHAPTER 1
SADIE
PRESENT

NO ONE SAID GROWING up was going to be easy. And with only days until my twenty-fourth birthday, it seems I've spent more than enough time figuring that out. Being an adult is definitely not my forte, though. That's pretty obvious.

I mean, why else would I be hiding out in my apartment, not answering my phone, or the buzzer to unlock the doors downstairs?

Because I've failed at being able to adult like normal people do.

And...my friends are trying to throw me a birthday party on Friday night.

I don't do birthdays. I don't attend birthday celebrations for other people, and I certainly don't go out and celebrate my own.

But Chelsea and Kelly are relentless. I swear, they've been alternating shifts between the two of them, taking turns calling my cell and ringing my damn doorbell. My refusal to answer only made them blow up my phone with text messages.

We're going out Friday night, Sadie. And you're going. It's your birthday. Get ready!

We've been friends since university, so for the life of me, I can't figure out why they haven't come to terms with my hatred for birthdays. Is it really so bad to detest celebrating getting older?

Another text comes in, and even though I roll my eyes, I slide my finger across the screen to read it…accidentally pressing the call button instead.

"No, no, shit, shit!" But it's too late. I can already hear the damn thing ringing, and Kelly answers on the second ring.

"About freaking time!" she exclaims.

I cringe as I hold the phone up to my ear. "I already told you guys, I don't do birthdays."

"Suck it up, princess. Because we're doing this one six ways from Sunday! It's Club Sin, Sadie! *Sin*! We have to go."

"It's just a club," I remark, but even I can hear the hint of intrigue in my voice.

Club Sin—or just plain Sin, as everyone calls it—opened downtown about six months ago. It's by invite only, which is weird enough, and no one can explain how or why Chelsea got an invite last week, making it even more mysterious.

The three of us are far from wild party girls, content to watch chick flicks on Saturday nights and order pizza from the local Domino's. We have our share of dates, but we don't take them too seriously. Mostly, because we can't. Have you ever sat across the table from a man who might look educated and handsome, but the moment he opens his mouth it's impossible to do anything but want to tune him out because you know he's laying it on thick and absolutely, positively full of shit?

That, to me, explains the entire generation of men I have to put up with.

It's not looking good for the future of mankind.

So, the idea of going to a club that's secretive as hell, where no one actually knows what happens beyond the doors, and where there are undoubtedly throngs of well-dressed, twenty-something boys pretending to be men…it doesn't bode well with me.

Especially not to celebrate my survival of another year of adulthood.

"Just a club," Kelly snorts. "And I'm just a virgin."

I chuckle wryly. "But you're not a virgin."

"And it's not just a club!" she exclaims, laughing. "You're going with me and Chelsea, whether you like it or not. It might be our only chance to find out if the rumors are true."

I sprawl out on the brown leather couch in my living room. "And what rumors would those be?" My gaze is locked on my sweatpants and bare feet. It's a day off from my job at my dad's surveying office, but it occurs to me idly that maybe I should put a little more effort into my appearance. You know, something other than gray sweatpants, a loose t-shirt, and the messy bun of sandy hair on my head.

"Which would you like to hear about first?" Kelly is practically bursting at the seams. "How about the fact that I heard there are orgy rooms? Like, rooms where multiple people can go in together and—"

"I know what an orgy is, Kelly." I stare up at the ceiling, pressing my lips together to hold in a sigh.

"Fine. But what about the VIP areas I heard about? Specialty rooms. You know, whips and chains…bringing the sexual experience to the next level, and all that jazz."

My eyebrow arches as I listen to her, but I scoff. "No offense, but it doesn't really sound like my kind of place."

"But it's Sin! We have to go, Sadie." She's openly whining now. "If you won't go because it's your birthday, at least come with us to help me out. I don't want to be the only one with Chelsea. What if she ends up in one of the VIP rooms with some smokin' hot guy, and I'm left fending for myself amongst the sea of dumbass guys there? I *need* you!"

I laugh, rolling my eyes even though she can't see it. "See? This is exactly why we should stay home."

"It's Sin!" Kelly repeats for the umpteenth time. "If I never get to go there because of you, I'll never be able to forgive you!"

I squeeze my eyes shut, still chuckling. "Oh my God, *fine*. But, I swear to you, Kelly, if I get there and you two ditch me for some kinky shenanigans going on in the back room, I'll never forgive *you*."

She knows I don't mean it, just as much as I know she will always forgive me, too.

"Deal." I can almost hear her smiling proudly through the phone. "Bring on Friday night!"

"I can hardly wait," I mumble.

But, I have to admit, a small part of me is anticipating this. A night of dancing, drinks, and letting loose. A couple hours to unwind with my girls, and then we can go home and resume our typical, sickeningly mundane lives.

"This is going to be a night we'll never forget, Sadie. I can feel it."

If only I'd taken her words for the warning they truly were.

———

Three days. That's how many days have passed in the blink of an eye, leaving me standing in front of the mirror now, wondering what in the hell someone is supposed to wear to a club that's known solely for its sexual mysteries.

I'd be lying if I said I wasn't nervous. It's just not my scene. Just going to Club Sin is all Chelsea and Kelly have talked about in the past few days, and their excitement and anticipation are infectious.

I *want* to go to Club Sin tonight—part of me does, anyway—but be damned if I'm going to admit that to my friends.

Either way, I'm still in my robe and slippers when the buzzer sounds throughout my apartment, announcing a visitor. A quick glance at my phone shows the text Chelsea just sent two minutes ago, saying they were in the parking lot, so I don't even use the intercom to confirm it's them. Instead, I just press the button, unlocking the doors downstairs, and wait for the click of heels and tittering voices to make it up the flight of stairs.

Sure enough, I hear Kelly before she even knocks on the door. I open it, and both girls stop talking immediately.

"You're not even dressed yet?" Chelsea says, wide-eyed, her eyes taking in my not-so-sexy ensemble. She's donning a sequined silver tank top and black leather-look leggings with knee-high boots, and Kelly's wearing a short red tube skirt with a flowy black top and the highest black pumps I've ever seen.

I know without even rummaging through it that my closet doesn't contain such over-the-top fashion items.

"I'm working on it," I reply, a hint of defensiveness in my tone as I turn away from the door and head back in the direction of the bedroom.

My friends are on my heels the entire way, and Chelsea pushes past me just inside the bedroom door. "Well, work faster. 'Cuz, Lord, help me, I feel a sin coming on!"

I laugh, rolling my eyes when she holds her hands up as though to announce, "Hallelujah!" This club has obviously really got her in a twist.

It's on the tip of my tongue to ask her or Kelly to pick something out for me to wear, but the request doesn't even get past my lips before they're both rifling through my closet and dresser drawers in search of the perfect outfit. If I'd been at either of their apartments, I might've been worried about what slinky little garments they might choose for me to wear, but seeing as we're at my place, with my relatively safe attire, I can't see how too much can go wrong.

Until Chelsea gives a dramatic huff, turns away from the drawer she's pulling clothing out of, and announces, "Thank

God I knew better! You never wear the kind of thing that shows off those curves, girl! So, I brought you something that will!"

I sputter and try to explain that I don't need her clothes, and that I can wear my own, but it's too late. Chelsea has already pulled Kelly away from the closet, and is pushing her toward the oversized purse she brought with her.

My chest constricts. If the entire outfit can fit in that purse…

"Here." Chelsea tosses a handful of fabric at me—and that's all it is; a handful. "Go put that on. Then, we can get a little mascara and smoky eyeshadow on that face of yours and get the hell out of here."

The moment I see myself in the bathroom mirror, with Chelsea's very low-cut, very short, and very tight strapless dress on, I know this night has already gotten out of hand. But when she spins me around and I see myself after she's spent fifteen minutes *sexing up my eyes*, as she calls it, I know there's no turning back.

The reflection staring back at me is a new woman, someone I've never met before. She's pretty…and *sexy*. And that's how I feel, sexy as hell.

Maybe this night won't be so bad, after all.

Hell, maybe me and my sexy eyes are made for Club Sin.

And there's only one way to find out.

CHAPTER 2
ASHTON

I KNOW I shouldn't want to do it, but I do.

Chances are, if you can't tell anyone about it, there's probably something wrong with what you're doing. But to hell with it.

Working at Club Sin *is* a sin. It has to be. If it wasn't, then people would know I work there. And I wouldn't have had to sign a nondisclosure agreement. And I'd have a goddamn job title.

But, no one knows I work there, I did sign an agreement, and I don't have a job title. So, I'm definitely doing something I shouldn't be.

But I like it. Fuck, I love it.

Being a part of a secret like Sin is exciting. Not to mention, the job itself is one I can't see myself ever tiring from.

I can't imagine ever working at a place like it on a full-time basis, because it could really start to play with your head, I think, but being able to go into Sin on Friday nights and do my thing is a welcomed break from the life-and-death shit I deal with at my *real* job.

I can't imagine what it would be like if my friends, family, and community knew what I did at Sin. If someone asked me what my job was there, what would I say? Fantasy maker? Sexual pawn?

Whatever you want me to be, is probably the most accurate answer.

Which is exactly why whatever goes on behind the doors of Club Sin, stays within the walls of Club Sin. It's unorthodox. Easily misinterpreted. And definitely not for everyone.

I certainly didn't think it would be for me. But, one night, and I was hooked.

And I can't think of one thing that could make me want to give up the gig I have there. Not one.

———

The club is packed tonight. Just wall-to-wall madness, a sea of patrons trying desperately to rid themselves of the trials and tribulations the workweek has thrown at them.

I can't blame them; it's the same reason I'm here, too.

Except that most of them are here only with the intent of drinking their faces off and being able to claim that they made it inside the velvet-covered walls of the club, gyrating on the dance floor to the beat of techno music and grinding with the barely-dressed dancers the club has hired to keep patrons hot and bothered.

Me? I'll be behind the scenes tonight.

As usual, I'm careful to park my vehicle in one of the parking lots a few blocks away, and keep the hood of my sweatshirt pulled down over my eyes, head down, as I make my way up the sidewalks and duck in behind the building that houses Sin. I press the passcode into the back door and slip in without a sound, as though I'm nothing more than a shadow.

"Where you been, Butler?"

I barely have the heavy steel door pulled closed before I see Chris poking his head out of one of the stockrooms, cases of liquor bottles stacked high on either side of him. Christian Tolman and his wife, Anya, own the club, and they run it well. All employees, whether they be waitresses, dancers, or even those with offices who work on the marketing and publicity of the club, are treated well. Like a family, as ridiculous as that may seem when referring to a club based solely around society's love of sex.

"I always worry when you're not here early, you know." A hint of a smile shows on his face, and he heaves one of the liquor cases down from the stack in front of him.

I lower my backpack from my shoulder and leave it by the door. "Then I really should start showing up on time like everyone else, instead of early," I smirk. "You're starting to expect it from me." I lift one of the cases up and carry it from the room.

"It's not so much that, as it is worrying about you and that career choice of yours." He hands another case over to me.

"You're worried about my other job, even though I come here once a week and put myself in danger of being manhandled by all these pretty women?" I don't even bother to keep the smile off my face.

"Yeah," Chris nods, chuckling. "That's got to be really rough on you, Ash. Now, shut the hell up and go get the room set up. Anya says there's a client for you."

"Already?" I crane my neck to catch a glimpse of the clock in his office. Barely ten o'clock. "Jesus, it's pretty early for *that*, isn't it?"

"Looks like you're a wanted man."

———

I get nervous every time I start a shift. I think I'd be crazy not to. There's no telling what kind of crazy woman will come through that door, or what she'll ask me to do. There's a waiver signed beforehand—she can change her mind at any time, and I can decline anything she asks of me—but still, there's something fear-evoking about being in a dark, locked room with only one other person and their fantasies to keep you company.

My job is simple—I'm hers for one hour. But the rules are just as clear: The room stays completely dark—she never sees me, and I never see her—and the conversation must continue throughout that one hour so that I can gauge how well the client—as we so eloquently call them—is handling the scenario.

In the five months I've been at Sin, not once has one of these one-hour sessions resulted in actual intercourse. It's risky, and a whole other level of intimacy for women—a level most women aren't comfortable with reaching.

But, there's been a whole lot of nakedness, touching, and breathless words.

Intimacy. That's what it seems to be about for the women who end up in the darkness of the Seduction Room with me. Yeah, that's what they call it. I let Chris and Anya know in no uncertain terms that I wasn't into all that bondage and fetishism stuff that some of the other specialty rooms were offering, but seduction?

Yeah, I can do seduction just fine.

And, honestly, my role has taught me more about how the female mind works than I ever could have known otherwise.

I'm a guy. And I like to get it on just as much as the next dude. But, I'm also not so completely delusional not to realize that women want that connection, that intimate moment that's just for them. They want to know that they matter, that what they want matters.

But, damn, some women are just hot little forces to be reckoned with, too. And their demands, whispered some-times with apprehension, but mostly with aching need, turn me on just as much as it does them.

But it's not about me. For that hour, I do—or don't do—

whatever my clients tell me to. And while I can't see them, and have no idea what they look like, I'd like to think I'm pretty good at recognizing voices. Removing such a vital sense such as sight from the equation tends to heighten the other senses, sometimes sending them into overdrive. Which is why I'm positive that I've recognized the same voices, and felt the same womanly curves—proving that I have repeat customers.

Which means I'm definitely doing something right.

Even if it is wrong.

CHAPTER 3
SADIE

CLUB SIN IS BUSY—BUSIER than I thought it would be, anyway. Somehow, my naïve mind equated the idea of it being by invitation only with it being smaller and more personal. And I guess it is, if you consider hanging out with more than a few hundred strangers to be personal.

This is a bad idea.

Something in my bones has been screaming that since we got in Kelly's car. Yet, here I am, surrounded by red velvet walls and very scantily dressed men and women who are delivering drinks while never missing a beat as their bodies seemingly move with the music that pumps from all corners of the building.

"This is going to be phenomenal!" Kelly shouts in my ear.

I turn to her, clutching my purse in my hands as though it's a lifeline. Her eyes are flitting from one side of the room to the next, taking it all in, never landing on one spot for more than a few seconds. Her excitement is coming off her waves, and, I'll admit, it's infectious. But, that doesn't mean I'm any more comfortable with the situation, either.

"Where's Chelsea?" She's no longer behind Kelly like I thought she was, and as I scan the room, she's vanished, her sequined top no longer visible in the sea of bodies around us.

Kelly is smiling like the damn Cheshire cat. "She went to inquire."

"Inquire about what?" I'm not even sure I want to know the answer to that question, judging by the wicked grin she can't rein in.

Kelly doesn't respond, just pushes me ahead, toward the bar. "Shots! That's what we need! Shots!" She chants the mantra the entire way, both hands pressed against my forearms to guide me toward the massive mahogany bar along the far back wall.

"I really don't think—" But she's not listening. And I also notice how she avoids my question.

Chelsea might be nowhere to be found, but Kelly orders up three shots of…what was that?

"Christ, Kel, what's in that?" I stare at the murky brown contents, my nose wrinkled in distaste.

"Doesn't look like much," she explains, lifting one of the shot glasses from the bar. "But it'll be your new favorite. For the birthday girl—the girl who will inhale coffee anytime, anywhere—I bring you the Wake The Dead shot. Tequila, coffee liqueur, and espresso." She hands the glass to me, waggling her eyebrows. "Not exactly my first choice, but it's not my birthday, now is it?"

She's right. I'd take my coffee any way I could get it. But with tequila? That's a new one for me.

"Take it, my friend," she laughs, and I finally pluck the glass from her fingertips. Immediately, she reaches out with her own glass and clinks it with mine. "Guaranteed to jack you up."

With those classy words, Kelly downs the entire shot.

I follow suit, letting the tangy burn of the tequila and the sweet, decadent taste of coffee slide down the back of my throat in one forceful gulp.

"Holy God, Kel! I've never drank coffee that burns before."

"First time for everything," she smirks, slamming the shot glass down on the bar dramatically. "Isn't that right, Chelsea?"

I whirl around to come face to face with my other friend, just as she tosses back the shot that had been waiting for her.

"That is exactly right," she grins. "And that's precisely what this night's all about."

The glint of mischief in her eyes unnerves me, and I grow cautiously still. I glance between the two women, my own eyes narrow and wary. They have something up their sleeves. "What's that supposed to mean?" I demand. "What's going on?"

Chelsea bites down on her bottom lip, barely able to suppress the anticipation rolling off her. She leans in close. "We got you a birthday present."

Normally, that would be a relatively safe statement, one that doesn't offer up anxiety and jangled nerves. But considering the way she says it, the way both of my friends have their gazes locked intently on me, and the fact that we're in the notorious Club Sin, her words scare the hell out of me.

"What kind of present?" I choke out.

I'm not sure if Chelsea can even really hear me over the reverberating bass of the music, but she must, because her eyes cast a glance away from me, over the crowd to the other side of the room.

An oversized sign, with gorgeous silver calligraphy writing on it, hangs from Victorian wrought iron bars above a door covered in silver tin tiles. The roaming red, purple, and white spotlights reflect off the damask pattern of it, making me squint as I decipher what it says.

"What's the Seduction Room?"

Chelsea gives Kelly a look, which must silently advise her that more alcohol is needed stat, because Kelly gives me a quick pat on the shoulder and turns away, signaling to the bartender.

"Whatever you want it to be, according to the very professional manager I just spoke with," Chelsea explains with a light laugh. But it's forced, I can hear it over the music and people around us. Even Chelsea is a bit nervous. For her, or for me, I'm not sure.

And that can't be a good sign.

"Ms. Mitchell?"

Both Chelsea and I turn, and a woman in a crisply fitted black designer suit with a dangerously low-cut lace camisole is standing between us and Kelly, who's finally got another row of shots poured in front of her. She turns, too, taking in the woman's classy outfit and meticulous makeup.

"That's me." I don't know why I say it. She obviously knows who I am, and she sought me out.

The woman gives me a reassuring smile, and an easy nod. "We're ready for you."

"Ready for—"

"Happy birthday, Sadie," Chelsea says, leaning against the side of my face to speak in a lower volume. "Go enjoy yourself."

Kelly looks slightly uncertain about their choice to send me off with the woman standing before us, but she shoves one of the shot glasses at me, wide-eyed and trembling with nervousness.

Without thinking, I take the glass from her. "Are you sure—"

I'm about to protest. Back out. Tell them all that this situation isn't for me.

But why? Because it's not part of my normal, mundane, safe routine? Hell, I don't even know what the situation *is*, and I'm already turning it down.

But the woman I'd seen in the reflection of my mirror earlier tonight wasn't that person anymore. At least, not right now. Tonight, that woman was fun, and adventurous. Maybe even wild.

We're ready for you, she'd said.

Well, I might not be ready, and I doubt I ever will be, but be damned if I'm not going to take this gift my friends have given me and at least see what it holds. With that in mind, I toss back the shot, push the glass back into Kelly's hand, and follow the woman in the designer suit.

"Time to open up that gift, ladies." I wink at my friends, sounding surer than I really am, and leave them standing at the bar, losing sight of them as the crowd of patrons fills in around them.

———

The sharply dressed woman leads me to the other end of the bar, away from the Seduction Room sign that my friends pointed out only moments before.

"We do everything in our power to keep things as discreet as possible," she explains, holding a door open for me—a door that was made to look exactly like the wall around it.

Ah, I get it. If I just walked into the Seduction Room using the door that opened onto the bar itself, everyone would see me go in, and see me come out. And secrecy was key, so Club Sin wouldn't allow that to happen.

She leads me down a darkened corridor, dimly lit only by sporadic security lights along the way. In my head, I'm questioning everything she tells me.

"My name is Lydia."

Is that even her real name?

"You do need to sign a nondisclosure agreement."

What kind of freaky shit is she scared I'm going to talk about?

"You can change your mind at any time, and don't need to say or do anything you're not comfortable with. You're in charge here."

Why would she feel the need to tell me that?

I'm absolutely losing my mind, only taking in about half of everything the woman is telling me. The nonchalant voice she's using with me isn't helping, as her calmness is only accentuating my frazzled nervousness even more.

I'm about to back out—after all, I'm in charge, right?— when something she says pricks at my consciousness.

"…but he's yours for one hour, Ms. Mitchell. Nothing said or done within these walls leaves these walls. That's what your friends bought you for your birthday. Freedom."

Freedom.

Be damned if that didn't speak to me on a level I wasn't quite ready to admit to.

We're standing outside a shiny black door, studded with chrome accents that seem to smolder like miniature flames, even in the dim lighting. She shoves the clipboard she's holding at me, and the pen. So, she was serious about the nondisclosure agreement.

I sign it without even reading the whole thing. Like I'd ever want to speak about this with anyone else, anyway.

"The room is pitch black, and it stays that way. Your identity is concealed, just as his is." She gives me a smile, surprisingly genuine considering the circumstances, then brings her arm up and glances at the watch on her wrist. "Your hour starts now. You're free to go in whenever you're ready. I'll be here in sixty minutes to lead you back out to the main club."

Lydia waves a hand toward the door in front of me. I would've laughed in any other context. The way she does it, like I wouldn't notice it without her help. But maybe that's how I appear right now—lost, and unsure where to go or what to do next.

With that, she turns away from me and heads back down the hallway.

I focus on the *click, click, click* of her heels until I can't hear it anymore, and then just stand there, staring blankly at the door.

Time is ticking, literally.

I can either stand out here and wait for Lydia to come back, or be a rebel and pull that damn door open. Even if I back out once I'm in there, at least I can say I tried.

Screw it.

I take a long breath, hold it, and let it out slowly. Then, I hook my fingers around the door handle and tug on it. It glides open easily, silent, and a quick peek into the room beyond it doesn't help me much. It really is absolute darkness.

No sound comes from the room, and even with the door pulled open practically the entire way, there's not enough light to give me even a glimpse of anything save for a few tiles on the floor nearest the doorway.

"You can come in. It's safe, I swear."

The voice makes me jump, startled. I must have been standing there longer than I realized, just staring into the darkness. I can't see him, but I realize he must be able to see at least my silhouette in the dim light. The thought is enough to make me take a step inside and pull the door closed behind me.

Even shrouded in darkness, knowing from the distance of his voice that he's obviously on the other side of the room, I can sense him. A sizzling pulse of energy that makes me blink, thinking I might be able to see sparks if I could just see through the blackness around me.

"I…" My arms are at my sides, my fingers pressed lightly against the door behind me. It's the only safety net I've got to cling to, keeping me oriented as to where I am in relation to my escape route. "I'm not sure…"

"I can tell," the man's voice says softly.

I can hear the faintest hint of amusement. I'm not sure whether to be relieved or offended.

"Will you tell me your name?" His voice holds no demand, just a suggestion, a bid to make me comfortable.

I shake my head, then realize how foolish that is. "No," I choke out. I clear my throat and try again. "No, I don't think that's a good idea."

"Fair enough."

I can hear him moving somewhere to my left, each step painstakingly slow and light. It occurs to me that I feel like I'm being hunted, and that I might not realize his impending attack until it's too late. Far too late.

"I hear it's your birthday."

The words make my throat constrict. "How do you know—"

"Easy," he says. "Your friends told Lydia, and she told me. That's all."

I nod again, rolling my eyes. Not only am I making silent gestures that no one can see, but I'm jumping to conclusions and freaking out, just waiting for this whole thing to be some kind of embarrassing setup. "Not till Monday, actually."

"Mine, too."

His voice is suddenly a lot closer to me than it had been, making it all the more difficult to focus on what he's saying. "What?"

"My birthday," he whispers. "It's on Monday, too."

"What are the odds…" I say absently, but I don't even realize the words are coming out of my mouth. Instead, all my senses are overloaded by the fact that I can feel his breath against my temple, and I gasp at the sensation of it.

"It's okay," he assures me. "You don't have to do anything you don't want to…it sure would be nice to have a name to call you by. Doesn't have to be your real one."

My hand is on my chest, and I can feel my heart pounding insanely under my fingers. "Rose." My voice is no more than a whisper. It's all I can manage.

Rose is my middle name, but most people don't know

that. Mostly because I hate the name, but I'm not too keen on feeling as vulnerable as I am right now, either, so I figure the name is suiting under the circumstances.

"Rose." The man's voice repeats it slowly, as though pondering it. And something in the way he says it makes me actually like the sound of it when it rolls off his tongue. "It's a pretty name," he adds.

I let out a slow breath, as slowly as I possibly can, hoping he can't hear me trying to level out my wildly beating pulse. "W-what's yours?" I roll my eyes in the darkness, feeling silly at my own obvious fear, then try again. "Your name, I mean."

His voice comes out in a seductive whisper, just a breath away from my ear lobe. "I think this is where I remind you that I'm whoever you want me to be."

I swallow hard, feeling my knees buckle slightly at the heat of his breath again my sensitive skin, and the artful persuasion in his voice. "It…it doesn't matter."

"Of course, it does," he offers. "This is your time. I'm on your clock, Rose."

He's doing it on purpose, I swear to God. He must be. Because there's no way his voice keeps coming out with that raspy quality, his breath touching my skin like a lover's caress in the most opportune places near my throat and just below my ears, without skillful knowledge of how to turn a woman on.

It's the Seduction Room, Sadie. Of course, he knows how to make you want him.

"May I touch you, Rose?"

The question catches me off guard. Not only because I don't expect his forwardness, but, in another sense, because he asks so damn politely. Up until then, I'm not sure I really believed I had a choice, even though it's been drilled into my brain since Lydia whisked me away from the bar. "I…I don't…"

My brain is screaming at me that this is a bad idea—that

being in the vicinity of a man with such a husky, sexy voice who wants to touch me and do whatever I want him to do…is a really bad idea. But my body is screaming louder, begging for me to give in, do something crazy, and take absolute advantage of the situation.

Oh God, this is what happens when you deprive yourself of—

"How about this?" His voice breaks through my racing thoughts, grounding me for a fleeting moment. "What if I put my hands on you—nothing crazy, just to make you feel something—and you can ask me questions while I try to calm you down a little, okay? We can stop at any time, but just give me a chance to ease that mind of yours a little, all right?"

I don't respond immediately, and he must take that as a sign. Either that, or he's decided to take a gamble, because I suddenly hear him shift slightly beside me, and his fingers slide gently over mine, still pressed firmly against the wall behind me.

His touch is surprisingly gentle in comparison to his deep, masculine voice, and the gesture makes my stomach clench.

"Focus on my touch," he whispers, but there's no demand in his words. "Feel me, and listen to me, Rose." His fingers graze the top of my hand, continuing to trail from my wrist, to the tip of each of my fingers, then back again. "Ask me something. Anything."

It's such a simple touch, nothing overly crude or aggressive or sexual. But my head is already leaned back against the wall and I can feel my breaths coming out in ragged, shallow pants. My eyes close instinctively, drinking in the sensation. "The darkness…why…"

His hand has migrated up my forearm, to my biceps, then my shoulder, his thumb massaging softly against the muscles. He's moved, in utter silence, and must be standing in front of me now, because his other hand is tracing up my other arm and shoulder, too. The realization is alarming—that he could move anywhere without my knowledge—but it's thrilling as well. "The darkness," he begins, "Is to keep our identities a secret. But it's also to create a sense of mystery. Not to mention…" His lips land ever so softly on my shoulder, and I gasp. "…being robbed of the sense of sight only helps to heighten the other senses. Do you feel that, Rose?"

He knows damn well I feel his lips brushing up against my skin as he speaks, and he's right; every one of my senses is definitely in overdrive. Oh my God.

I want him.

It doesn't make sense, it's irrational, and it's downright reckless to even think about it. But, damn, do I want him. And I'm pretty sure he knows *that*, too.

"What usually happens…" My breath hitches at the sensation of his teeth grazing boldly across the curve of my shoulder. "In this room, I mean. Do you…*fuck* everyone that comes in here with you?" Just being able to verbalize the question boldens me. I've never been a fan of the 'F' word, but what else could you really call it when you're in a room with a complete stranger you can't see? Christ, his touch and the couple shots I've had are loosening me up a bit, it seems.

He doesn't answer right away. Instead, his lips kiss tenderly along the side of my neck. At first, gentle, with featherlight pecks. Then, his tongue, warm and sensual, joins in, sucking and tasting me, making me inhale sharply.

"Almost anything can happen in this room, Rose," he explains, never once missing a beat as his kisses land on my skin in time with my heartbeat. "But, no. I've never fucked anyone in here. Although, I'm not opposed to it, to be honest."

It's pitch black, but I can feel him grinning like a mischievous teenager.

The thing is, if he keeps kissing me like *that*, I'm not sure I'm overly opposed to it, either.

Christ, what is wrong with me? Where have my morals and self-respect gone?

They're safely tucked at home, that's where—right along with my jogging pants, boring life, and nonexistent love life.

Tonight, I'm not safe and sheltered Sadie Mitchell...I'm Rose. And she's wild, reckless, and free.

"How much time do we have?" The question falls from my lips just as I reach forward in the darkness, for the first time feeling the warm, bare skin of his chest.

I can't breathe. *Oh my God, is he naked?*

Daringly, I let my fingers trail down the chiseled contours of the side of his abdomen, and let out a sigh of relief when my fingers find the edge of a belted pair of jeans. *He's not naked. At least, not yet.*

"Lots of time," he breathes just before nipping at my collarbone with his teeth.

I gasp again, and I'm not sure my legs are going to hold me up much longer.

"Good," I pant, giving in. "Because, if you're not opposed, then I want to be your first."

CHAPTER 4
ASHTON

I'M the last person who should be discussing what's right, what's wrong, and where the boundary is between those two things. Hell, my boundary is probably in a completely different spot compared to where other people would draw the line.

But the moment I put my hands on Rose, I know without a moment's hesitation that this next hour with her is going to be completely different than any other hour I've spent in the secluded darkness of this room before.

The girl is trembling, first of all. And I'm not so callous as to not notice that she's keeping herself close to the exit door on purpose, probably ready to bolt the first chance she gets. I've been alone in this room with many women, all jittery and buzzing with alcohol and anticipation, but never a girl who is so obviously terrified to even be here.

And that's all I've been thinking of her as, too—a girl. She seems young—younger than me, sure, but young in the sense of shyness and inexperience, too. This isn't her scene, and I know from Lydia's description that it wasn't her idea to come here. Her friends have brought her here in celebration of her birthday. They bought her an hour with *me* as a gift. And when you put it like that, I suppose I should see the humor in it.

And maybe I do. At least, that's until it dawns on me how scared she is of me. For the first time ever, it occurs to me to leave her standing there in the darkness and disappear out through my own exit door on the other side of the room to go seek out Lydia, advising her that I have standards, and there's no way I'm going to try to seduce a young woman who obviously doesn't want to be seduced in the first place.

But then, two things happen.

First, I touch her. Not a mild pat on the back, but a soft graze of my fingertips up the warm, smooth skin of her bare arm. The way her skin feels under my touch, combined with the sound of the resultant gasp that falls from her lips—something changes. She isn't just scared, then. She's enticed.

She wants me.

And by the time her own exploring fingertips rake down my abdomen, making me ache with relentless need, I fucking want her, too.

That's when the second thing happens.

She *asks* me.

Okay, so it's not actually a question. But that's probably why it affects me so much. She'd seemed so timid, so uncertain. Then, she took a chance, put her own hands on me without seeking permission, and said the magic word. Want. I *want* to be your first.

Oh, Rose. Suddenly, I want the same damn thing, but for completely selfish reasons.

Mostly, because I don't have to ask *her* for it. And her sudden flash of confidence is intoxicating as hell.

"You can have anything you want," I say, and I'm surprised to hear the waver in my voice.

As I duck my head again to continue my sensual assault of tender kisses along her bare shoulder, Rose turns her head, just enough to push me back slightly...and just enough to align her face with mine.

In that moment, I can feel her breath, hot and damp against my skin. For that entire moment, neither of us moves, teetering on the precipice of desire and lust, sharing the same thin air but feeling deprived of it in some way, unable to take in what we need. Because air isn't our most vital necessity, and other more urgent desires are churning within us.

"Kiss me." It's meant to sound like an instruction, but my words come out as more of a plea. It's the first time that I've demanded something within the confinements of the Seduction Room, and it breaks all the rules I'm supposed to follow.

But rules don't matter. All that does is the fact that Rose doesn't hesitate to obey, and her lips crash against mine with a fervor that my lust-filled brain can't completely comprehend.

After that, everything becomes a blur of gasps and panting and touching that rivals anything the walls of this room have ever seen before. I'm on her, a wild animal on its prey, with her back pressed up against the wall. Having her pinned there, with my weight pushed fully against her, I know she can feel how fucking bad I want her. All of her. There's no denying the painful hardness I've got pressed up against her abdomen.

My tongue invades her mouth, exploring her, teasing her, and she matches each feverish kiss and lick relentlessly.

There are no words uttered between us.

Because they aren't needed.

Only two people with an emptiness inside them—the need to fill a deep void within themselves—would understand the unspoken conversation between us. I recognize her desperation for what it is.

The craving of freedom, in any sense that she can obtain it.

Oh, Rose, I crave it, too. I want to tell her I understand, that

I feel that way, too. That I truly believe everyone craves true freedom in different ways.

But, be damned if I will ruin this to call her out on her deepest fears and insecurities. That's not what this is about. If it's a moment's worth of freedom she wants, I'll give it to her the only way I know how.

"Rose—" I whisper.

"Shh," she pants. I feel her head tip back, and listen to her gulping in air. "Don't ask," she hisses through her sharp breaths. "I'll stop you if it's not okay."

I bend forward, nipping at the skin at the hollow of her throat. "I wasn't going to ask anything, doll, but that's good to know." I chuckle against her throat. "What I was going to say was that you taste like spiked coffee."

The sweetest sound I've ever heard meets my ears—she genuinely chuckles. Then, I can feel her grind her hips forward, eliciting a guttural groan from me that I can't contain. "Wake The Dead," she whispers, as though it's a big secret.

"What?"

"Wake The Dead," she giggles again, leaning forward to find my lips again and kiss me—an act of tenderness now, not primal hunger, which shocks me. "It's the name of the shot I was drinking. My friends said it's guaranteed to jack you up."

I hold her bottom lip between my teeth, then kiss her back, harder. I can't help myself. She has yet to stop the slow, painfully delicious rolling of her hips, and it's doing all kinds of fucking insane things to my brain. "You're jacking me up, all right."

"You like that?"

I have to jut a hand out against the wall and bite down on my bottom lip when she slides a hand between us and runs her fingers along my erection that's straining achingly against my jeans.

"Like is not a strong enough word," I bite out through clenched teeth.

"Are we running out of—"

I fumble in the dark, but my fingers find their way to her lips, silencing her. "Time?" I finish for her. "You're too focused on the time, doll. I won't let us go over our allowed time limit, and I won't let someone walk in here and catch us. You're safe, okay?"

With my fingers still pressed against her lips, she nods. But without warning, I feel her tongue against my fingers, then her mouth surrounds them, sucking gently.

Fuck. I'd give anything to see her right now.

She lets her teeth graze up the length of my fingers as she releases them, and I have to clear my throat. This girl is killing me. Just fucking killing me.

"I...I..." Rose clears her throat. "I do want you. I know I shouldn't, but I do."

"Want, huh?"

She's motionless. "Want is not a strong enough word."

To hell with this, and to hell with my niggling thought that this might actually be a mistake. "What you want, you get," I remind her in a raspy voice. "In this room, that's how it works."

"Can you sit down somewhere?"

Her request only stops me for a moment. The woman's got a plan. And if that isn't hot as hell, I don't know what is. "Trust me, okay?" I whisper, kissing her hard again. Then, I tug her away from the wall, leading her further into the room.

I know where everything is, how the entire room is set up. I should, seeing as I helped to determine the layout. But Rose has got me all flustered and all I can think about is burying myself to the hilt inside her, and fucking her until her body clenches around me. Which is exactly why I stumble onto the armchair in the corner, practically falling into it with an unceremonious "Oompf!"

"Shit, sorry," I choke out.

But it doesn't matter what I'm saying, because I can feel her hands tracing across the edge of my jeans, doing a little fumbling of her own as she tugs at my belt buckle.

"You say we have time," she mutters. "But my mind is racing, and so is the clock. Don't let me waste another minute, please."

The way she says it, it makes me wonder if she's actually talking about wasting another minute of *this* hour, or in general. But, it's really difficult to ponder life's bigger questions when a woman is unzipping your jeans.

"Whatever you want, Rose. I mean that." And I do.

She says nothing as I let her pull my jeans down slightly, lifting my weight slightly to help. It's the first time that the absolute darkness around us feels obstructive and daunting to me. I'm used to it—focusing on the feel of a woman's touch, the sensation of her soft fingers mixed with the pulsing and throbbing of my cock. At least, I thought I was. Because, now, I want to see her as her hand encircles my shaft, and I want to witness the sexy little 'O' her mouth makes when she realizes how thick and long I am.

For now, all I can do is feel my erection spring free and, without hesitation, her hand holds me against her palm. A loud groan escapes my mouth just as she inhales sharply.

"Oh, fuck," I whisper without meaning to.

"Yes," she replies with a shaky breath. "*Exactly.*"

I don't know what she means by that…until the pressure of her hand on my cock disappears and I think she's changed her mind. That's when her lips find mine, as she's crawling onto me, straddling my hips with her knees pressed against either side of me.

Without thinking, I slide my hands up her arms, hold her steady, and push her gently back. It's enough to get her attention, which is proving hard to do. She's got an agenda, or maybe it's something to prove. To herself, or to me, I'm not sure, but there's something. Which is why I stop her.

"Rose." I start with her name, just so I can be sure she's truly listening. "Are you sure about this?"

There's a moment of silence, but it's short. "God, yes."

Once again, I wish I could see her eyes, to see how much hesitation lies within them.

Instead, I reach one arm down beside the chair to a stand I know is placed there, and I fumble aimlessly for the drawer. Inside it, I pull the small square packet from the drawer and press it into her hand. "Then we're going to need that."

For a second, there's no sound or movement. Hesitation; I can recognize it even without seeing it.

But, then, in a flurry of movement, I hear the packet being ripped open and her hand is wrapped around me again, and the sudden pressure of her fingers pulls a sigh from deep within me.

"I want this." Her voice meets my ears, soft but assertive.

Shit, she's going to do me in long before she means to, if she's not careful. And if she wants this, I want to give it to her...but, hell, not *yet*.

"Easy does it," I say, coaxing her into slowing down a bit. "Your touch is definitely getting my attention, which I'm sure you can tell." I let my head tilt back as she rolls the condom onto my length, soaking in the sensation. "How about you tell me what you want from me, doll. I want to hear it from your mouth, because I can't see it in your eyes."

Her fingers are gripped tightly around my cock, her hand sliding up and down, making my breath come out in ragged breaths.

"I want..." Her mouth is so close to mine that I can feel her breath against my lips. "...to not have to ask for it. You're a man, and you know how this works. I want..." Her body shifts, and her free hand finds mine, guiding it down between her legs. "…to feel you kiss me, feel you move against me, and feel you *fuck* me."

She gasps when my fingers pull her panties to the side, then pull her tight dress higher up on her hips. Her demands are turning me on, and I can feel the damp heat emanating from her against my palm. This woman is ready, waiting, and she wants me.

I want her, too.

Which is exactly why I waste no more time, using one hand to trace up her body to the back of her neck, pulling her face to mine and crashing my mouth onto hers, and the other to encircle her hand that's still wrapped around my erection, guiding it to her entrance. There, I halt, giving her the last possible, fleeting idea of a chance to back away.

She doesn't. Instead, she arches her hips as she lets go of me, lowering herself onto me. Shamelessly, I lift my hips just slightly, too, meeting her movements and burying myself within her.

Rose's guttural moan is lost somewhere amidst our kiss, but the sound does something to me. There's no way to remain objective when a woman is straddled on your lap, riding you with a primal desire unmatched against any previous sexual experience you've ever experienced, and her feverish kiss and relentless hip thrusts are making it even more impossible to keep my wits about me. But, there's something about the way she's caught my attention—it's more than just a blatant physical urge to fuck her senseless. That's what she's asking me for, but for the first time in all my time at Club Sin…I want to know *why*.

My hands crawl up her body again, and I pull at her strapless dress, first tentatively, then more aggressively. Rose doesn't try to stop me, and I pull it down the rest of the way, freeing her breasts and rolling her nipples between my thumbs.

She lets out a loud gasp, followed by a breathless "Oh

God…", which only makes her roll her hips harder against mine. At this angle, I can't possibly be any deeper inside her, and the heat, and sensation, and slick wetness of her is driving me absolutely insane.

I can't think, and if I could see, I know I wouldn't be seeing anything clearly, either.

Jesus, she's the one fucking me senseless.

"Rose…" It's said with a muted warning, because if she keeps going, rocking her hips up and down my cock like that, driving me into her so recklessly, I'm not going to last another minute.

"Fuck, yes…" The words pass her lips, caressing mine like a blissful hum. She's lost now, captivated only by the desire to come completely undone from the inside out.

And I need to give that to her.

With one swift movement, I guide a protective hand around to the small of her back, holding her in place as I push myself forward. Instinct kicks in, and Rose's thighs clench around mine, holding herself to me as a startled shriek emits from her mouth.

In an instant, I lay her down on the floor in front of the chair as gently as I can manage. There's a bed in the room, in the far right corner, but I know I couldn't have made it there. Not when I need to make her come as badly as I want to.

"What are—"

"Shh," I hiss, hovering above her. I thrust hard into her— once, twice, and then again, picking up speed. "Let me fuck *you*, Rose. Take it. Take what you need."

Her legs wrap around me, and her hips rock upward, meeting each thrust in perfectly matched synchronicity. She gasps each time I bury myself inside her, her nails digging painfully into my shoulders as she takes the mix of pleasure and pain without complaint.

"Your name…" Her words are but a plea, begging me. "What's your—"

"Ash," I growl, slamming into her again. "Ash—"

"Oh God, Nash!"

Rose shatters beneath me, every muscle within her clenching around me as she screams my name again. She's so tight, so deliciously wet. I thrust into her wildly, again and again, but I can't hold back anymore, and I'm tipped over the edge, finding my own violent release only moments after her.

I curse loudly, giving in to my climax, letting my mouth find hers again to muffle any further crass words falling off my tongue. I begin to slow my movements, taking my time to allow both of us a moment to catch our breath and allow the euphoria to subside.

"Holy shit," I chuckle, my voice hoarse and barely above a whisper. I've already broken one of my own rules, usually being sure to at least say the client's name as she gets me off, in a bid to make her feel wanted. But, damn it, there's a big fucking difference between a woman giving me a hand job and a woman…doing whatever Rose just did to me. I'd lost all train of thought, and my mental checklist of personal rules along with it. "That was incredible, Rose," I breathe, my weight resting heavily on my elbows as I hover over her. "You are—"

It takes me a moment to realize she's pushing me off her, and I pull away, rolling onto my side to give her the space she's silently asking for.

"Rose?"

I can hear her shuffling about, fabric being pulled back into place and breaths being let out slowly as she tries to compose herself.

"Rose," I say again. I reach out in front of me as I pull my exhausted body onto my knees, then stumble to stand, but my hands find only air.

"I…I…oh God," she stammers, somewhere to my right.

Fuck, I'm disoriented, but I reach out again. She's not there.

"I shouldn't have…" Her words drip with mounting hysteria. "Oh God…"

"Rose. It's—"

All I want to tell her is that it's okay, that she just needs to calm down. All I want to do is touch her again, put my hands on her, and ease her mind and body after the moments we've just shared.

But, I can't. Because it occurs to me a moment too late that she's made it to the door, and the crack of dim light that shows as she opens it isn't enough for me to catch a glimpse of more than her hourglass silhouette. As my eyes adjust, I can see her bend at the waist, and it occurs to me that perhaps she's searching for a light switch. Either way, it gives me the time I need to get to her, and I attempt to stumble toward her while pulling my jeans back up.

"I shouldn't have done this."

Her words hit me at the same time the door closes, and I reach out hoping to catch it before it clicks, but it's too late. Far, far too late. Because she's on the other side of that door, the door I'm forbidden to open, and she may as well be a million miles away.

CHAPTER 5
SADIE

UNTIL FRIDAY, I thought I'd made some bad choices in my life. You know, stupid, reckless, childish decisions that all teenagers and young adults make—the choices we make, learn from, and move on from. The stuff we laugh about later when we're older, and wiser.

But, now that it's Sunday morning, and I'm still lying in bed, staring at the ceiling in an aimless stupor, wondering what the hell was going through my mind on Friday night when I did...*that*, I know with absolute certainty that screwing Mr. Seduction Room wasn't just a bad choice.

It was the worst choice. Ever. Not only had regret immediately washed over me the moment it was over, but knowing that I'd done something that I could never speak of in regular conversation—that was the definition of having done something that was beyond reckless. I'd been impulsive for the first time in my life, edged on by the slinky dress I'd borrowed, and Chelsea and Kelly's eager support, and I'd given in to the hype of the situation.

Everything Nash had said in his sexy, raspy voice, and every single touch he'd offered me with his strong but tender hands had only fueled the fire inside me. A fire that I hadn't realized had been quietly smoldering away within my core until he'd unleashed it.

He'd made me feel alive, made me feel desired. Hell, he'd made me *feel*.

But that didn't make what I'd done any less wrong.

As promised, Lydia and her designer suit had been waiting for me on the other side of that door—the door I still can't believe I'd been able to find in my state of shock and exhaustion and utter inability to process what I'd truly just done—and she'd said absolutely nothing, her face stoic and expressionless. But I'd known damn well she'd heard me only moments before, gasping out Nash's name, and the thought only made my face burn hotter with embarrassment. I couldn't look her in the eye—just like I couldn't look myself in the eye when she'd led me into a tiny bathroom, word-lessly giving me a moment to freshen up and compose myself.

In the mirror above the sink, the woman who'd looked back at me wasn't me at all. My hair, once meticulously styled with Chelsea's curling iron, was now a disheveled mess, and may as well have screamed, "I just fucked some guy in a dark room down the hall." And my eyes, though still lined with makeup, looked haunted, and guilty as hell. Rightly so, I thought.

After that, Lydia had stayed silent while leading me back down the hallway, taking a different corridor than the one I'd been led down on the way in—I thought it was, at least, but my sense of direction could've been off, though hopefully not as badly as my judgment—and I was led out into the bar once again. Sure enough, I was on the other side of the club completely, nowhere close to the door I'd disappeared into, and nowhere close to the Seduction Room sign.

I found Kelly and Chelsea easily, still camped out in their

spot near the bar, one with a vodka cooler in her hand and the other still downing shots like it might be the last one she'd ever get to have.

Chelsea, being the adventurous one, was wide-eyed and squealed with delight at the mere sight of me, begging with a drunken slur to know every raunchy detail. Kelly, who'd obviously been nursing the same drink the entire time I'd been gone, could see it written on my face that explaining was the last thing I wanted to do right now. She'd given Chelsea a look, which seemed to register in her intoxicated brain, and Chelsea just nodded.

Kelly drove me home then, never once asking any of the questions that must have been plaguing her mind.

Both of them slept over at my apartment though, staying all of Saturday, letting me divulge the truth a little bit at a time while Chelsea got over her hangover and vowed to never drink again.

Even now, two days later, I'm not sure I'll ever forget the way I looked after that hour spent at Club Sin. And, seeing as I did admit to my two friends that I did, in fact, screw Nash, I'm just as sure that I'll never be allowed to forget that, either.

"Nash. That's kind of a hot name, though, right?"

Both women are curled up on my living furniture, hanging on every word I say. Kelly reaches across the arm of the couch and gives Chelsea a smack on the arm. "I think you're missing the point, don't you?"

"I'm just saying!" She rubs her arm gently, scowling. "Okay, fine. So, neither of us actually expected you to screw him, I'll give you that, Sadie. But, damn, it's hot! Think about it. On your birthday, you had sex with a smoking hot, muscular dude in a completely dark and mysterious setting. At Club Sin, no less! And you never have to worry about seeing him again, because you never actually saw him in the first place!"

Kelly looks on the verge of hitting her again, but I hold up a hand, halting her. "It's fine, Kelly. I know what she's trying to say. I just…shouldn't have done it, that's all."

"Why?" Chelsea challenges me. "Because it was ballsy and totally unexpected? Girl, I'm not saying to go fuck random dudes in clubs on a regular basis. But you were spontaneous, and you did something you normally wouldn't do. Don't beat yourself up over it. Live a little, hmm?"

"I think I did a whole lot of living in that one hour, thanks." I stand up, unsure where I plan on going, but needing to do something. "It was just a stupid way to do it. That's all I'm saying."

"And it was just hot. That's all *I'm* saying." Chelsea purses her lips in defiance, daring me to say otherwise.

I roll my eyes, but a faint smirk tugs at the corner of my mouth. "Maybe he's not hot at all, Chels. You ever think of that? I've never seen him."

She plucks the pillow from the armchair she's sitting in and tosses it at me. "Oh my God, are you serious right now? It's over, Sadie! Now, all we get to do is analyze the situation to death and dream about the hottie. He's hot, got it? In our heads, Nash is hot. Besides, how can he not be smoking hot with a name like Nash?"

I steal a glance over at Kelly. "There really is no hope for her, is there?"

"None." Kelly holds her hands up in surrender. "She's a lost cause."

"Shut up, both of you." She laughs, dramatically swinging her legs over the arm of the chair. "I happen to be a hopeless romantic at heart."

Kelly and I just stare at her, our mouths partially open.

Chelsea sighs. "Well, I am! I just happen to really love the idea of a hot, half-naked man whispering in my ear and letting me call the shots while I save a horse and ride a cowboy."

My cheeks flame bright red. Leave it to Chelsea. "You're relentless," I say, looking away.

It's her turn to hold up her hands. "I just call it how I see it. Sounds like a damn good birthday, if you ask me."

"I didn't," I snap, once again too humiliated to keep my tone in check. But I see her face falter slightly, and immediately feel bad. "Anyway, speaking of birthdays. You two are both coming to my parents' house with me for the dinner tomorrow night, right? I can count on one hand how many of these formal family get-togethers I've gone to over the last few years, but I can't get out of it. Our neighbors are going to be there."

"The infamous Butlers?" Chelsea's face perks up.

I point a finger at her. "Just because I've told you everything about them, doesn't mean you can show up there tomorrow and bring it all up. Got it?"

Chelsea glares at me, appalled. "What am I going to say, Sadie? *Hey, is that the asshole that you had a crush on when you were a kid that acted like a dick?* Give me some credit."

"That's exactly what I think you'll say," I admit, unable to hide my amusement. "I'm just begging you not to. Please?"

"Best behavior, I swear." She holds her hand over her heart.

"Your best behavior still makes us worry," Kelly interjects, making me laugh.

Chelsea shakes her head. "Just answer me this. Is he still hot?"

"Who?" I wrinkle my forehead in confusion.

"The neighbor you had a crush on! Focus, Sadie."

I bend down and pick up the pillow she'd tossed at me, throwing it back. "I told you, I haven't seen him in years."

"This should be fun, then." Her devious smile makes my stomach turn.

"In case you haven't realized, we're not exactly kids anymore, and we don't exactly live with our parents. And

Ashton is even older than we are, so he won't be there. I told you, it's my parents' friends that are coming over. I never said anything about Ashton Butler showing up."

"A girl can always dream, can't she?" Chelsea gives me a wink, shrugging.

I give up. Kelly's right, she's hopeless. And the truth is, I've found myself thinking about Ashton far too many times over the years, wondering and waiting to see if he'll show up at the family barbecues and events my parents hold at their place. I've truthfully only attended a handful of them since I moved out, preferring to keep the prying questions and wistful comments about my lack of a love life at bay, but not once has Ashton ever graced us with his presence at any of those gatherings. He's always too busy, according to his parents.

But, Chelsea's right. A girl can always dream.

———

I'm far more nervous about this damn dinner than I should be. Hell, it's with my family; just my brother and my parents…and our neighbors, who may as well be family, too, considering how often they're around. People who know me inside out and backward.

Except, they don't. Because I highly doubt any of them would guess what I'd done on Friday night, and I know for certain that none of them would ever be able to handle it if they found out.

I'm Sadie Mitchell, Daddy's little girl and Mommy's little angel. And in their eyes, I'm not grown up, still a bouncy little ten-year-old with pigtails and a Barbie Corvette in tow. Gunner, my brother, sees me no differently.

I've also spent my teenage and adult years doing as I was told. Taking the courses in high school and college that were suggested to me by my parents. Graduating with a boring business administration diploma and heading straight over to my father's company to work for him, as recommended by him. Hell, I even rented the apartment my parents liked best, because it looked out over the city from the fourteenth floor, and because it was safer than a ground-floor unit. You know, because my parents said so.

So, to say that they wouldn't expect Chelsea, Kelly, and I to frequent a place like Club Sin would be an understatement. To say that they would never believe that I'd have casual sex with someone I couldn't even see—even thinking about it might give my family a communal aneurysm right then and there.

Thinking about it was giving me quite the headache, too. But I can't stop thinking about it. Each time I close my eyes, I can feel the way his lips felt crushed against mine, the way every curve of his muscles felt under my own fingertips. And, each time, I gasp, my eyes snapping open as I realize how much my body is craving him again.

Maybe I don't regret it as much as I initially thought I did. There might be parts of it that I wish I hadn't gone through with—like the fact that I chose a complete stranger that I couldn't see to experience my first taste of sexual freedom with—but there were definitely parts that I couldn't bring myself to regret, too. Like the fact that I hadn't known what it was like to feel like that with someone, to allow someone to have me in the most intimate way possible without having to face their judgmental eyes and personal preferences and desires. That night had been about what I wanted, yet, I couldn't help but feel that Nash had gotten what he wanted as well.

Nash.

I've been saying his name over and over in my head since the moment I escaped from that room. And that's exactly what it was, an escape, because if I'd stayed any longer and allowed him to say something to me after what we'd just done together, he'd have ruined it by giving me a harsh reminder that it was a business transaction, nothing more. My friends had paid for him to pretend like he wanted me.

Christ, when I think about it like that, it all seems even worse. What was I thinking?

That's just it, I hadn't been thinking at all. No analyzing, no scrutinizing, no exaggerated contemplation. I'd just done it. Done *him*.

And, now, all I can think is that I pray to whoever might be listening that my sexual encounter with Nash isn't hanging over me like a neon effing sign the way I think it is, because I won't be able to handle it if my family finds out about it.

———

"Sadie! You girls are late, as usual!" My mother calls from the kitchen before I've even got the front door closed.

"Traffic was bad," I lie, knowing full well that she'll know it's not the truth. I kick off my shoes, tucking them in beside Chelsea's, who has already disappeared in the direction of the kitchen. She's a sucker for my mom's cooking, and I don't blame her. Having a mother who knows her way around a kitchen better than Betty Crocker herself definitely had its perks while I was in college, and saved me from countless nights of eating frozen pizzas and mac and cheese from a box.

The truth is, I dragged my feet after I got home from work, and Chelsea and Kelly had shown up to pick me up before I was ready to go. I'd tried a few excuses as to why I couldn't— or shouldn't—go, but Chelsea wasn't listening to me. Mostly because she wanted the home-cooked meal, I think.

"Chelsea, darling! So glad you could come."

I trudge into the kitchen, seeing my mother embracing my

friend like she's her long-lost daughter. My parents love both Chelsea and Kelly, which I guess is a good thing. Good, solid, level-headed young ladies, as my father calls them, who are currently pushing a wine glass into Kelly's hand before the greetings are even finished.

"Wouldn't miss it, Mrs. Mitchell." And Chelsea's not lying when she says it, because I know she'd have left me at home and come by herself if I'd refused for much longer.

"Enough with that Mrs. Mitchell stuff, hmm? It's Anna, dear. Now, Rick, get this girl a glass of wine while I finish up with the garlic alfredo sauce, please." She gives Chelsea a pat on the shoulder, smiles affectionately at Kelly, then turns back to the stovetop, her own wine glass in hand, picking up the conversation she and Mrs. Butler had obviously been having before we arrived. I didn't notice her sitting there, a stool pulled up near the oven as my mom works away, the two of them tittering over some gossip column they'd read in the newspaper that day. I give her a little wave, smiling at both women, but choose to follow my dad into the pantry, where he's in search of another bottle of wine.

"Glad you could make it, Sadie Baby." My dad stands up from where he's crouched, eyeing the vast selection of wines that are displayed along one wall of the pantry, and leans in, kissing my cheek tenderly. "Didn't know if you were feeling up to it, seeing as you seemed a bit off today at the office."

Immediately, I feel guilty. I had been off today at work, choosing to keep to myself and just focus on my duties of answering the phone and getting some invoices sent out, instead of making small talk with Dad and singing along with the radio like I usually did. "Sorry, Dad. I'm just tired, I guess. Thought you would've appreciated not having to hear my tone-deaf singing for one day." I smirk, and so does he, but the smile doesn't reach his eyes.

I'm such a bad liar.

"You'll never hear me complain about you being there," he smiles, handing me the bottle of wine. "Even if you are tone deaf."

"Oh, one point for Dad," I laugh, raising my hand to make a stroke in the air, mimicking keeping score. "Be careful, I'll get my retaliation soon," I add, turning away from him to head toward the cupboard for glasses. That's the thing with my father—my whole family, really. Everything is so easy with them. They never harp on me very much about anything, and everything is always a game, a joke, or light-hearted banter. Then again, maybe I've never given them a reason to give me a hard time, and maybe it's the constant teasing manner that irks me most. Maybe part of me yearns to know what it's like to have parents who feel compelled to admonish me for something. Or, maybe I want to know what it's like to have done some worth being admonished for, as messed up as that is.

For the thousandth time that day, Nash and his sexy voice and tantalizing fingertips enter my mind, and I remind myself that I *had* done something worth being scolded for, and I don't ever want them to know about it.

"Where's Gunner?" I ask as I pour the wine for Chelsea and me, trying hard to push Nash back into the deepest depths of my mind. I don't overly like wine, and I certainly don't appreciate it the way my mom and dad do, but I would have a glass with them...just because I know they like that.

"He's upstairs," my mom explains, just as a deep voice announces, "I'm right here."

I turn at the sound of my brother's voice, a genuine smile on my face as I hold one of the wine glasses out to Chelsea. I hadn't seen him in months, and we'd always gotten along well, so the sight of him should have been a welcomed surprise.

And it *is* a surprise I get when I lay eyes on him. Well, not on him, exactly. It's the tall, muscular man beside him that catches my attention and turns my stomach inside out.

"Ashton." His name falls from my lips in a breathless whisper, my smile faltering as I struggle to process the sight of him after all these years. He *is* a man, too. A lot of man. Taller than Gunner, and broader in the shoulders than him, too, Ashton Butler is as ripped as any man could be. The curves and contours of his muscular arms and chest show through his black t-shirt, and his jeans are worn with utter perfection, as though made just for him.

He is breathtaking, and the collective intake of breath beside me indicates that Chelsea and Kelly wholeheartedly agree.

"Well, hey there, Sadie." Ashton's mouth twists up at the corners, watching the three of us as we stare at him.

My mouth is hanging part way open, and I quickly clamp it shut. *Smooth, Sadie. Real smooth.* "Uh, hey," I choke out. Clearing my throat, I try again. "How's it going, Ashton?"

My cheeks are burning up, and I hate that both his parents and mine are watching with amused grins, like this is some kind of reality show and we're tonight's entertainment.

"I'm good," he chuckles, nodding his head toward me. "Are you planning to drink that bottle all by yourself, or do you think you'd be willing to share?"

Stifled laughter ensues around me, only making me blush a deeper crimson color. I lower my gaze to the wine bottle clutched in my finger, staring at it as though I can't figure out how it got there. "Crap, yes. I'll share, I mean. Sorry." I stumble over my words as I hold the bottle out to him, not daring to take the steps forward to bring it to him in case I stumble over my own feet just as badly.

Ashton takes the bottle, his gaze never leaving mine. "Thanks."

I wish I could bring myself to look away, but I've been teleported back to my teenage days and I feel like the schoolgirl crush I had on him in elementary school hasn't dissipated like I thought it had. If anything, it's just exploded wide open and multiplied into a living, breathing, heart-crushing entity of its own.

There's no getting Ashton Butler out of my head now. Of that, I'm certain.

CHAPTER 6
ASHTON

WHEN GUNNER MITCHELL sent me a text on Saturday, inviting me to his parents' place for dinner on Monday night, it'd completely slipped my mind that it was my birthday. At the moment I'd received it, I'd been distracted by my job. My real job, that is.

Not the one that led me to my rendezvous with Rose.

But, every other moment since Friday night, it's been her that I've been distracted by. The memory of her breathing, her initial hesitancy and ultimate submission to her needs, the way she'd kissed me like she'd known me forever, like it mattered…

Like I mattered.

I was having a hard time letting go of Rose.

Maybe that's why I agreed to go hang out with his family, and my own. I'd never been one for the camaraderie between our families, unable to figure out why we couldn't just be the Butlers, instead of the Butlers and Mitchells combined. But, for the first time in a while, I had two consecutive days off from work, and the idea of mindless distraction and a little family time did sound good.

So, I agreed to show up. I was even pretty happy about my decision.

Until right now.

Because, now, I'm not just happy about it. I'm fucking ecstatic.

I haven't seen Sadie Mitchell in years, which is partially my own fault for avoiding our families like the plague, but there's no denying that she definitely isn't the annoying little teenager I remember.

Because Sadie isn't just all grown up. She's hot.

Hell, she's fucking beautiful. And not just in that dressy, heavily made-up way that so many girls depend on to look sexy. Sadie's standing in front of me in jeans and a fitted Nike t-shirt with not an ounce of makeup on her pretty face, her hair tumbling down past her shoulders…and she's downright gorgeous.

Judging by the shell-shocked expression on her face, I'd say she likes what she sees when she looks at me, too. So do her friends, and the identical expressions the three of them are wearing have me struggling to bite back my laughter.

Women. If I were so obvious about checking her out, they'd be disgusted with me and calling me a pig. But there they are, undressing me with their eyes unabashedly.

I steal a glance toward my mother, arching an eyebrow, but she's just watching with a mix of humor and something that might resemble pride. Awkward.

I resist the urge to shake my head, choosing instead to clap my hands together in the hopes of breaking everyone out of their trance. "So, dinner smells good. What's on the menu?"

I knew without a doubt that the meal would be fantastic. Anyone within a five-mile radius of this house, and who's ever attended the community potlucks in our subdivision knows damn well that there's no one who can rival Mrs. Mitchell's cooking. Sorry...*Anna*, as she's been trying to get me to call her all night. I've just never got the hang of that one. She still sees me as a kid, and I still see her as my best friend's mother.

What I don't expect is that neither Sadie nor her friends talk to me throughout the entire meal. I don't exactly try to initiate conversation, either, but that's mostly because I can't get a word in edgewise. Nothing has changed over the years —if you put my parents in a room with Rick and Anna Mitchell, there is still no shortage of conversation.

A buzz sounds from my pocket, and I look down. Perhaps I only heard it because I felt the vibration of my phone, because there isn't even a hitch in the conversation as I dig the phone from the holster clipped to my belt, glaring at it.

"Are you on call?" My mother asks me.

The conversation has died abruptly, and I realize that all eyes are on me. Well, to be honest, I've noticed that Sadie and her friends have been glancing my way quite often over the course of the evening, but this is the first time she's looking at me with a piqued interest instead of her gaze just flitting over me in hopes that I won't notice.

"No," I reply to Mom, shrugging. "I just still get notifications for fire calls even though I'm not scheduled for tonight." I press ignore on the text screen after reading through the information, and tuck the phone back into my pocket. "Sorry about that. That was rude to pull out my phone in the midst of such a great dinner." I nod in apology toward each person at the table, lastly to Mrs. Mitchell. "Thanks, Anna. You really outdid yourself."

Anna waves a dismissive hand my way, and I swear she blushes as she pushes her plate away. "Now, now. No need for apologies." The woman stands, grinning. "Besides, I haven't even served dessert. You haven't seen anything yet."

She tosses her cloth napkin onto the table and begins to clear away some of the dishes. "Black forest cake. Anyone want coffee with it? I know Sadie does."

Sadie smiles graciously up at her mother, but her eyes only leave me for a split second. "You're a firefighter?"

I nod, relieved that she's finally opened up a line of conversation with me, and I'm about to respond when I pick up on something her friend—Chelsea, I think?—is giggling about to Sadie's other friend.

"…need to get Anna to turn that coffee into those tequila shots we were tossing back the other night…" She's chuckling like a schoolgirl, her voice low enough that I know the comment is meant only for their ears, but I lean in anyway, thankful my own mother has followed Anna into the kitchen, and my dad and Rick are engrossed in their own chat about the NHL game they watched last night.

"Coffee and tequila?" I interject, my voice suddenly huskier than it had been only moments before.

Maybe it's my own paranoia kicking in, but Sadie suddenly looks more on edge. Her friend, however, is all too keen to elaborate.

"Yeah," Chelsea grins mischievously, matching my pose as she leans across the table, too. "Coffee liqueur and tequila with espresso. *Wake The Dead*, I think they called the shot." I can tell she's enjoying having my undivided attention, but each word she offers me is making my head spin in a nause-ating spiral. "Damn good stuff," she adds in a whisper. "Especially if you like coffee the way Sadie does, right?" She gives her friend a playful nudge, but Sadie isn't seeming to find the humor in it.

Neither am I.

I can barely breathe, and flashes of Friday night are hurtling through my mind at a dizzying speed.

It's my birthday, but not until Monday.
Wake The Dead.

I press my palms against the tabletop in an attempt to stop the room from spinning. What else had she said to me?

Chelsea is laughing now, amused that Sadie's giving her a warning glare. "What? Those shots were good. Guaranteed to jack you up, right?" She chuckles even louder, and Sadie's hand jerks slightly, hitting her friend under the table.

"Shut up, Chels," she says with forced laughter, her smile coming out more as a grimace.

Oh my God. Oh. My. God.

I can barely form a coherent sentence, and I can see Gunner out of the corner of my eye, one eyebrow arched high on his forehead. I must look as sickly as I suddenly feel. "Where'd you guys have these shots?" I choke out. "Never heard of 'em."

"Ow!" Chelsea cries, glaring at Sadie now. "Why the hell did—fine!" She sighs dramatically, turning back to me. "At a bar. We took Sadie out for her birthday."

"It was nothing," Sadie speaks up, but her tone tells me that it was the furthest thing from nothing. "Just a few shots, then we went home," she explains needlessly. Unfortunately, her guilt-ridden features and incessant need to downplay it are creating more of a reaction than she would have received if she'd just stayed quiet, but her vagueness and unease tells me more than I wished to know.

This isn't happening.

My mind is wielding a thousand thoughts around, and I'm chaotically bouncing between wanting to push my best friend's little sister in the other room and demand to know where she'd been on Friday night, and wanting to throw up the meal her mother had just fed me.

Because I already know where Sadie Mitchell was that night. There are too many coincidences in that short-lived conversation for the truth to be anything else.

She was on my lap.

I fucked my friend's sister, unknowingly. And at Club fucking Sin, no less.

Hysteria is quickly kicking in, and I'd laugh at the situation if Gunner wasn't staring at me so damned suspiciously.

Oh my fucking God. My own sin catapults through me like a vile disease, spreading heavily into my limbs, gut, and mind, rendering me speechless. All I can do is repeat it over and over again in my mind, because to say it out loud would make it even more real.

I had sex with Sadie Mitchell, and Gunner's going to crucify me if he finds out.

But, that's not the worst of it. The next thought that comes quickly in the wake of the first is even more terrifying, and so dangerous that it has me standing abruptly and excusing myself while I duck out of the room and head straight for the bathroom down the hall.

I had sex with Sadie Mitchell, and I'd give anything to do it again.

CHAPTER 7
SADIE

I WATCH Ashton bolt from the table, the haste of his actions making me flinch, startled.

What was his problem?

"I'm not sure why he's rushing out of here," Chelsea whispers in my ear. "But I do love to watch him go."

I scoff at her comment, rounding on her, my words thankfully hidden by my mother's reappearance with the cake and coffee carafe in her hand. "Are you nuts? I thought we agreed to never speak about Friday again?"

Kelly stays quiet, but Chelsea rolls her eyes. "I wouldn't have said everything. It's all fun and games. Relax, will you?"

It's my turn to roll my eyes, pulling my napkin from my lap and tossing it onto the table. With a brisk smile at my mother, who's cutting the bakery-worthy cake into slabs big enough to feed an army, I tilt my head toward the living room. "I'm just going to go out to Kelly's car to get my phone, Mom. I must have left it out there. Besides, it's stuffy in here, and I need some air. I'll be right back."

No one protests, and my steely glare must be clear enough because neither of my friends attempt to follow me.

The air outside is chilly, cutting through my t-shirt and

making goosebumps rise on my skin. Rubbing my bare arms with my hands does little to defend myself from it, but I pad down the driveway in my sock-covered feet anyway, pulling the passenger side back door open to search for my phone.

Kelly's car is a mess. I don't know how she finds anything in here. For a girl so organized and neat within her own home, the chaos of her car's interior makes me think she must have some kind of Jekyll and Hyde thing going on.

It's muffled, but I think I hear the creak of the front door, followed by a faint click as it closes. Perturbed by the effort it's taking to find my phone, I call out, "I thought I said I'd be right back." Chelsea never did quite master the art of subtle hints.

But it's not Chelsea's voice that meets my ears. "I need to talk to you, Sadie."

I gasp, mortified by the fact that only my ass and legs are visible from the opened car door, and I'm very, very ungraceful as I crawl backward out of the backseat, my phone in hand.

"Happy Birthday to you, too." It's meant to be a joke, but no humor stares back at me from Ashton's cool, dark eyes. He looks back toward the house, and his uneasiness stirs something within me. "What's wrong?"

I'd have found it amusing that he ducks in behind the opened car door—he can't possibly believe it could hide his broad, muscular body, right?—if his movement didn't result in him being so close to me that I can smell his cologne, bold and intoxicating as it invades my senses. I'm forced to look up to meet his gaze, pressing my shoulder blades against the car.

"Look, I don't have a lot of time before someone notices I came out here, but—"

"Why would that matter?"

"Just listen, will you?" he snaps. "I need to know where your friends took you on Friday night."

Thank God it's dark outside, leaving only the outdoor light fixture on the front step to illuminate the fast-growing blush that's rising in my cheeks. "Like hell you do," I say evenly, immediately regretting it. A defensive answer like that will only result in more red flags being raised.

I sidestep, planning to go around him and leave him standing there alone, but his arm juts out, propping himself up against the door. "What club did you go to?"

"What's gotten into you? I haven't seen you in years, and now suddenly you want—"

"That's the funny thing about seeing, Sadie. We don't really need to. I've learned something about seeing. If you can't see, then the rest of your senses become heightened, making you hear and taste and feel more acutely. Did you know that?"

My blood runs cold, and I'm afraid to move. My breath seems to have caught in my throat, strangling me.

"Seems I've got your attention now," Ashton says grimly. "And I know why. Because you *did* know that. Because you found out on Friday night."

Somehow, a gasp falls from my lips, and I reach out to grasp the car door for support. *Don't say it*, I plead silently. *Don't say what I think you're saying.*

"Because I told you that…on Friday night." Ashton's voice is quiet, and I realize that he's just as humiliated as I am.

Club Sin was supposed to be one night of fun. Of freedom. One secretive night that no one else ever had to know about. This couldn't possibly have gone more wrong.

"You…" I choke out. "You're Nash…"

"Ash, actually," he explains. "But I didn't think it was a good time to correct you, all things considered."

Heat flames my face, and I open my mouth once, twice, giving up on the third time when no words come out.

"I won't tell anyone, Sadie." Ashton's movements are

slow, and his index finger touches my chin so lightly I can't be sure he's actually touching me until he's tilting my face gently up. "And I hope you won't, either. But—"

"But? But what?" My knees are weak beneath me, the fire in his fingertips carries the ghost of all the other touches I've experienced with him only days before.

"But…I'm sorry." His eyes are on me, looking into mine like he can see into the deepest depths within me. "I'm sorry for the way things happened between us…" His teeth bite down on his bottom lip, and the sight ignites something inside me. "…and I'm sorry for this."

Before I can process what's happening, Ashton Butler's mouth is on mine unapologetically, his tongue dancing, warm and wet and delicious, with my own.

A sound comes from somewhere in my throat, but it's a halfhearted protest at best, and stifled by his kiss.

He pulls away just as suddenly as he descends on me, his eyes a mix of wild and wary, conviction and uncertainty.

"I don't know why you were there on Friday night, Sadie, and it's not my place to ask. But, damn it, we can't change what happened between us. And I don't want that to be the end of it."

I stare at him, wide-eyed. "You don't—"

"I might be at Sin every Friday night, but you need to believe me when I tell you that I've never done *that* before. That I've never felt that before. You're in my head, and I can't get you out of it."

I'm dumbfounded by his confession, my mind a minefield of thoughts and emotions just waiting to explode.

"I—I can't do this," I stammer, lifting my hands to his chest to push him away. "It was one stupid night. A stupid decision." I raise my gaze to meet his. "A stupid mistake."

Ashton steps to the side, and I'm thankful for that. I know damn well I'd never be able to make him move if he didn't want to.

"It wasn't a stupid mistake, Sadie." He sounds like he's begging me, but I'm not sure what for. "We all do crazy things. But we aren't kids anymore. Or teenagers, for that matter. That's just life—day after day of crazy shit that we do, say, or make ourselves believe so we can get through it as adults. But, sometimes, things happen for a reason, Sadie."

I stare at him for a long moment, and our eye contact only breaks when I become convinced that I see the curtains move in the front window. When I turn, they're still again, but my paranoia is now running rampant.

"Sorry, *Ash*," I say. "But this isn't one of those things."

Then, I move away from him, aware of the chill once more as the heat from his body dissipates from my skin, and I walk silently back toward the house, just as my mother opens the door.

"Sadie Rose Mitchell, you're in just your socks! You'll catch a cold!"

CHAPTER 8
ASHTON

IF I'D HAD my jacket with me, I'd probably have jumped in my truck and peeled out of that driveway, worrying about the apologies I'd need to extend toward the Mitchells later.

But I'm at a loss, unsure what to do next. And the only thing I do know is that I'm not prepared to walk away from Sadie just yet.

It's funny how things change so fast. One minute, we're kids, annoyed by each other, desperate to drive the other one insane. The next, we're standing in her parent's kitchen and I'm completely enthralled by how fucking beautiful she's become.

And the next, I find out how beautifully we fucked.

If I didn't know any better, I'd say the universe is getting a pretty good chuckle out of all this.

I duck back into the house, but Gunner cuts me off just inside the door.

"Where were you?"

I hold up my cell. "Bathroom, then I stepped outside to call into the hall. Not used to being off the clock, I guess." I grin, but it's forced.

"You weren't out there with Sadie?"

Fuck. Suspicion laces his every word.

"Yeah, she was getting something out of the car while I was on my phone."

Gunner lets the silence ensue, and each passing moment of silence twists my gut even tighter. "Is there something going on between you and my sister, man?"

"What? Hell no," I spit out. "How can you even ask me that?"

"Simple. You took off like a bat out of hell, all jumpy and shit. And she came back inside looking like she's upset. And you were both outside in the front yard." His eyes bore into mine, and I see his jaw clench once, twice. "So, I'm going to ask you again, Ash. Is there anything going on between you and Sadie?"

I stare at him, knowing I'd be certifiably insane to tell him the truth. That'd be as good as a death sentence. He's always been protective of Sadie, and not even a lifetime of friendship would break that. Finally, I shake my head. "No way, Gunner. There's nothing happening between me and your sister."

Which is the truth—there isn't a damn thing happening between us now.

Because it had already happened.

Us. Her and me. We'd 'already happened' four ways from Sunday.

But, Sadie made herself clear. Anything between us was past tense. One night. Nothing more.

We were over before we'd begun.

————

The rest of the week passes by without incident. I don't hear from Sadie—not that I would expect to, as she doesn't have my cell number or my apartment number, as far as I know—but I also don't hear from Gunner.

Not that it's out of the ordinary. He's got his life, and I've got mine. We're not exactly adjoined at the hip the way we used to be back in high school. But there's not a word at all from him. Not even when I attend a massive fire call on Wednesday night; a fire that results in the death of one victim and the hospitalization of two others. The fire made news headlines due to the casualties and destruction, yet I never heard a word from my friend.

Gunner almost always checks in to see if I'm all right following a fire of that magnitude. A simple text, at least.

But a text never comes.

That's because he fucking knows I lied to him. We've been friends forever, and we can usually read each other like a book. So, not only are Gunner's suspicions warranted, but if he's wary, it's only because he truly feels there is a reason to be.

And there is.

Because, until Monday night when I came around the corner and set my gaze on Sadie for the first time in years, I'll be honest, I hadn't given her a second thought. She was just a kid in my mind—the annoying little sister Gunner and I could never seem to steer clear of.

But, now that I've laid eyes on the grown-up version of that little girl, the blue-eyed, naturally pretty brunette with the luscious curves and creamy skin, I want to do the complete opposite of steering clear. I want to know her. I want to make her smile, and I want to know why her eyes don't sparkle with the contentment of a happy, successful woman. And I want to be the one to make them sparkle.

That's how I felt *before* I realized she's the one I'd been with on Friday night.

Now, I have even more questions, and even more desire to see what's really between us.

Because there is something between us. I knew it when I thought she was Rose, and I know it now. Putting together the woman I'd had the amazing night of sex with in the safety of that darkened room, and the woman that had stopped me in my tracks with her beauty the moment I saw her—the combination is more enticing than anything I've ever imagined.

Enticing enough to make me want to cancel my night at Club Sin tonight. Not only tonight, but permanently. For the first time since I met Christian and Anya, the owners who offered me the gig at Sin, I don't feel the allure and anticipation of going into the Seduction Room and doing what I do.

Part of me has always known there's something wrong about having casual encounters with multiple women in secrecy, and part of me has known there's something wrong with me for wanting to do it.

But, until now, I've never had even a sliver of a reason not to want to.

I have no one waiting at home for me, and I have a job that causes me to put my life on the line every damn day. Don't get me wrong, I love being a firefighter, and my crew is like family, and living that life is my choice. But, sometimes, having an outlet to step away from that life and just break things down in the basic, primal needs of a man and a woman is necessary, not to mention welcomed.

But since finding out what I know now—that Sadie came to Club Sin and unknowingly ended up acting out her own fantasy with me—the only thing I want to welcome into my life is the chance for her to do it again.

Because since last Friday night, Rose has been in every fantasy I've thought about, and Sadie in every one since then.

I don't know what that means—for me, for her, or for us—but I'd give anything to find out. I just wish she would, too.

CHAPTER 9
SADIE

THIS IS EXACTLY why most people don't do crazy and outlandish things. Most people with a brain, anyway.

Because things go wrong. Things blow up in people's faces, and they're left looking like a fool and not knowing how to fix the totally messed-up situation they're in—a situation they should've never been a part of in the first place.

Yet, here I am, humiliated, scared, and nowhere close to knowing how to move on after what happened.

I screwed Ashton Butler. I didn't mean to—I mean, I *meant* to, but I hadn't known it was him at the time; it wasn't supposed to be *him*!—but I'd allowed myself one stupid and foolish night of fun with my friends, and it turned into what could possibly be the most embarrassing thing I've ever done.

And the worst part of it all? It was amazing.

Ashton has been all I can think about all week. You'd think it would be the flashes of memory from that darkened room that would be careening my thoughts directly into the gutter—the way his fingertips seemed to know right where to graze to make me sigh, or the way his hips moved with mine, a synchronized, instinctual rhythm that had set my body on fire.

But, no. It isn't our night together that's having the most breath-stealing effects on me at all.

It's Ashton's kiss. His mouth on mine while we stood in my parents' driveway, a silent, animalistic promise that he isn't just attracted to the thought of Rose, an unseen woman who'd played the part of a seductress with fiery need running through her veins.

He wants *me*. I'm not Rose, and I'm not who he expected me to be. Hell, he couldn't stand me when we were kids, and he didn't try to hide that fact.

I've never felt that before. You're in my head, and I can't get you out of it.

But, now, he wants me. And I don't understand it.

Because, the truth is, I want him, too.

But there's one little difference.

I've always wanted Ashton Butler. Before I was even old enough to know what that means, I'd been enthralled by him, despite his disdain toward me.

We were just kids, though. I know I probably bugged the hell out of him, being a typical preteen girl with a crush on an older boy. And he was my brother's best friend, just as irked by my presence as Gunner was.

I'm sure it's a right of passage for all little sisters. At least, I'd like to think it is.

Either way, a lot has changed between the Ashton and Sadie we were ten or fifteen years ago.

I stare at the Pepsi can on my coffee table beside me, beads of condensation sporadically dripping from it onto the coaster underneath. I've barely moved from my couch since I got home from work, and I've managed to avoid both Kelly's and Chelsea's calls. I haven't been able to bring myself to tell them the truth about who Nash really is, or about Ashton's kiss and confession in the driveway. Between my father's prying bids to make sure I'm okay throughout the workday, and my friends' constant badgering to find out what's going on during the evening, I'm about two seconds away from telling everyone to mind their own business. They can go deal with their own lives, instead of standing by and watching the train wreck that mine has become.

The problem is that, while they have the chance to look away, I don't. I can't pretend I didn't do what I did, and I can't ignore the fact that I feel what I feel. It's a never-ending loop of thoughts in my head—what Ashton and I did, the things he said, how different we are.

And, we are *too* different. Right?

It's not the first time that I realize that I'm the one making excuses as to why this would never work. The funny thing is, we've never even discussed what we *do* want, and yet I'm convinced it's destined for disaster.

I'm my own worst enemy, it seems.

I stare at the Pepsi can again. *Rose would never destroy something like this before it even started.* That's the thought that keeps floating to the surface of my subconscious, too. If I took a chance and became Rose last Friday night, why the hell can't I find the strength to take a chance and see what becomes of this whole mess?

I know exactly why, but be damned if I want to admit it out loud.

Just thinking about the reason, though, is enough to make me sit up and shake my head at my own weakness. There's only one way I'm ever going to know if Ashton and I are too different, if there's even a chance of things working between us. And there's only one way I'm ever going to know if my stupid decision on Friday night was actually worth the humiliation and suffering it's caused me since.

If Rose got me into this mess, she could damn well get me out of it.

———

The dress I'd borrowed from Chelsea last Friday night seems tighter tonight, somehow, more restrictive. Like the body I'm trying to squeeze into the strapless ensemble isn't the one that it's meant for.

Because it isn't. I'm not Rose, I'm definitely still Sadie. And this dress isn't meant for me. If it was, I wouldn't be tugging at the skirt of it, trying unsuccessfully to make it an inch or two longer, and I wouldn't be wobbling like a newborn calf in these godforsaken high heels.

Rose is gone, and she seems to have taken with her any confidence we'd shared.

Unlike last Friday, I don't have an invite to Club Sin, and I'm not with anyone who does. But, with a little cajoling and a whole lot of stammering and awkwardness, I manage to at least get the bouncer at the door's attention.

"If you just tell Lydia I was here last weekend, she'll remember me." *I hope.* "I really need to talk to her. I'm Rose. Er, Ms. Mitchell." It occurs to me that I don't know whether my friends had provided my real first name to her or not, but hopefully with the mention of Friday night and the last name she'd used to address me, I can at least jog her memory and somehow get the chance to convince her to talk to me.

People are babbling and complaining behind me, but it's too late now to turn around and leave. The bouncer turns slightly away from me, speaking in a hushed voice into the miniature microphone near his shirt collar. I take a moment to compose myself, tugging my hand through my hair, which I've left loose but haven't curled as fancily as it'd been the previous week.

Out of the corner of my eye, I see movement. At least, I think I do. Not in the lineup behind me, and not near the clusters of people laughing and hollering around us. Near the wall of the building. But when I focus my full attention on the spot I thought I saw someone, they're gone, disappearing around the corner.

Stop it. You're just paranoid that someone will recognize you.

Besides, it could be anyone. Someone who'd stepped away from their circle of friends for a cigarette, one of the staff members on a break, someone with—

"Miss? Ms. Mitchell?"

I swing around, and the bouncer is glaring at me impatiently.

"Lydia says to go on in. She'll meet you inside the doors."

CHAPTER 10
ASHTON

THIS FEELS WRONG. I shouldn't be here. And as I enter through the back door of the club, I know why.

Because my thoughts are monopolized by Sadie, and my time would be better spent tracking her down and trying to talk things through with her. It's the only chance I have left. Avoiding what happened between us, pretending like it never happened at all, isn't going to make it any easier on either of us—yet, that's exactly what she's doing.

I get it, I do. The way things started between us last week; it was unorthodox, to say the least.

But, damn it, something still started. We can't undo what we did.

And I sure as fuck can't forget about it.

Yet, here I am, back at Club Sin despite every synapse in my brain telling me that I shouldn't be.

Which is exactly why I head into Christian's office first, before getting ready to take over my role in the Seduction Room.

"You're even earlier than usual," he smirks, glancing up at the clock. "How's it going, Ash? I heard about the fire a few days ago. Saw it on the news. You okay?"

The mention of the fire makes my throat thick, and I swear I can still feel the smoke choking me and burning painfully as I breathe it in. "I'm good. It just, you know, puts things in perspective, I guess." I lower my backpack to the floor, and the thud it makes is the only sound I can hear in the office save for the distant booming of the dance music making the walls hum with vibration from the main room of the club. "Which is something I'd actually like to talk to you about."

"The fire?" Chris's brows arch in askance.

"No," I say, shaking my head. "Perspective."

———

I'm just reaching up over my head and pulling my t-shirt off in the locker room when Lydia's voice floats through the air from the doorway. She won't come in, unsure if I'm dressed or not. Like almost everyone else that I frequent within the back hallways and rooms of Club Sin, she's seen me shirtless, though, so it doesn't faze me at all to come around the corner and meet her gaze.

"You looking for me, Lydia?" I ask, knowing she must be as there's no one else in the room. "What's up?"

"Are you on the clock yet, Ashton? There's a...client waiting."

Shit, they're coming here earlier and earlier every week.

"Yeah, sure. I wondered why you'd scurried off in such a hurry." She'd ended up in Christian's office about a half hour ago, and I was surprised at how much her insight into everything I'd spoken to my boss about had helped me. Perspective. From a woman's vantage point. Maybe that was the difference. I gave her a halfhearted smile. "I'll be there in a few minutes if you want to send her in."

She seems hesitant, and I wonder if she's about to say something further. But she finally nods, turning to head back down the hall.

I reach out a tentative hand, touching her shoulder. "Are you okay? Is something wrong?"

It's Lydia's turn to offer me a weak smile. "Fine. Just thinking about your conversation with Chris," she admits. "I'm glad that...I mean, I hope things turn out the way you want them to."

I don't know why, but the way she says it, mixed with the faintest hint of a smile on her face, makes my forehead wrinkle slightly in confusion. But I don't have time to question her further.

There's someone waiting, and even though my heart's not in it, I know that I made a promise to Christian in his office tonight. And I always keep my word.

"Me too, Lydia. Me too."

———

I only have to wait in the darkness for a minute or two before the door across the room opens and the dim light of the hallway washes across the first few tiles of the floor nearest the doorway. Only the faintest hint of the woman's silhouette is visible, and I have to squint my eyes, intently concentrating on the outline before me.

She's wearing a tight outfit—which is the norm in a sexuality-fueled place such as Sin—and her hair is long and straight, cascading past her shoulders.

The door closes quickly, though, and any chance I have of seeing any more of her attributes is extinguished.

"Hello," I say encouragingly, my usual charming tone sounding hollow to my own ears.

I shouldn't be here, I think to myself for the hundredth time today.

"Come here." The woman's whispered beckoning hits me with the force of a tsunami. She speaks too quietly for me to recognize her voice, but there's something about the cool, confident tone that sparks something within me.

Familiarity.

I obey, taking a few steps. By my estimation, I'm in the middle of the room. I hear shuffling, movement, and the slight click of her heels…then nothing.

Silence takes over, and I find myself straining to hear something—*anything*—in the darkness. "What are—"

"Shh." Her voice is close enough that every muscle in my body clenches. I don't expect her to be there. That's what that sound had been; she'd taken her shoes off, taking away my opportunity to follow her through sound alone.

"I need to know something," she whispers in a sultry voice, and I take in a sharp breath as I feel her fingertips, bent so that her nails graze along the contours of my abdomen, trailing across my skin as she moves silently around me.

I feel suddenly like she's stalking me, hunting me with a predatory instinct.

That voice…

"What is it?" I reply, my voice husky and coarse. "I'll tell you what you want—"

The fingertips are suddenly on my lips, shushing me. Her accuracy astounds me, like she knows exactly where my mouth is in relation to hers, like she can see me but I can't see her.

I'm the blind one in this room.

"Tell me," she breathes, her breath hot and damp on my jaw, "Did you know that being robbed of one sense only heightens the others?"

Her finger moves away from my mouth and I'm about to say her name, but her mouth is on mine in a heartbeat. I'd recognize that kiss anywhere. The delicious sensation of her tongue against mine, the way her mouth fits against my own as though custom-made for me…

And the intoxicating taste of coffee and tequila on her lips.

A growl emits from deep in my throat, and I'm on her within seconds, guiding her backward as my body pushes her across the room, up against the wall. My hands roam every inch of her body that I can find, and if I wasn't absolutely certain it was her before, I do now.

Sadie.

It takes every ounce of control I have to break that goddamn kiss, but I do it, letting my head press against her forehead as we both pant loudly in the looming silence.

"What are you doing here?" It comes out more of a plea than a question.

"I needed to know…if you were serious." She can barely catch her breath, and I find some pride in knowing that breathlessness is caused by me.

"Serious? About what?" Fuck, I wish I could see her eyes.

"About me."

Her words take me aback, but then I resist the urge to chuckle. "And did you just get your answer?"

I'm not a betting man, but if I were, I would bet every-thing I had on the belief that I can hear her smile in the darkness.

"I could *feel* the moment you realized it was me," she admits.

"I told you, robbing one sense only heightens the others," I tease. "I wish you'd start believing me."

"But what about when you rob me of all my senses?" she chuckles. "Because you do. I lose all sense when you're around."

"That's exactly how I felt the moment I saw you standing there in your parents' house, Sadie. You're beautiful," I confess, my thumb coming up to caress her cheek. "So, when I realized that it was you—"

"I'm not the girl you met on Friday night, Ashton." Her jaw stiffens beneath my hand. "I mean, it *was* me, but I don't —this isn't something I do."

"One night," I whisper. "That's all it was supposed to be, right?"

She nods against my hand, remaining silent.

I lean down and kiss her again, this time more softly. "And who do you think I wanted two minutes ago, Sadie? It's not Rose The One Night Stand I want right now," I say. "It's you."

"But you're here," she says cautiously. "Back in the Seduction Room. I can't compete with that." She clears her throat. "I won't."

The idea that she'd even think I'd ask her to should offend me, but I'm also enamored by her willfulness and insistence that she won't put up with it. This woman is stronger than she gives herself credit for. "I'd never expect you to, Sadie." I lower my face to hers, nuzzling her jaw just enough to elicit a soft sigh from her. "I came here tonight and told the club's owner about you. I told him I'm done, Sadie. I respect the guy, and wouldn't leave him with no one to cover the room tonight, but this is it. I won't be coming back after tonight. I'm walking away from Club Sin, in hopes that you'll give me a chance."

She's silent and unmoving, presumably processing the weight of what I've just proposed.

"And what if I won't?" she asks.

"Doesn't change the fact that you came in here and made me see that there's more to what I want in life than anything Club Sin could offer me. I'm done with this, and I won't deny that it's the connection I feel with you that's the catalyst for my decision."

"If I tell you I'm not interested in being with you, you're still—"

"Yes, Sadie. I'm still leaving Sin." I can't contain my laughter. "Now, please tell me why you're still pretending you don't want to be with me, and yet you shrugged that sexy little body of yours into that dress and came back here to find me."

"Because…" She seems unsure of the right words to say. "Because I want you."

I sigh with relief at her admission, even though it doesn't answer my question. Nothing she could say would sound sweeter on those luscious lips of hers. "There. Was that so hard?"

"Yes."

"Why?"

"Because I've wanted you since I was a kid. This just seems unreal. We can't—"

"You've wanted me since we were kids?" My mind is reeling.

"How could you not know?" she laughs. "I did everything I possibly could to be near you, all the damn time…"

"I noticed *that*," I say wryly. "But I didn't know you—"

"Had the biggest crush on you in the history of adolescence?"

"Wow, I'm sorry, Sadie."

"You should be. You were a total asshole to me when I was younger. Do you remember my twelfth birthday? You yelled and swore at me and everything."

I do remember, and I'm not proud of it. Hell, Gunner even brings that day up every now and then, purely because of how cruel I was. "Yeah, I remember. I'm pretty sure your devastated expression and quivering lip have been etched into my mind since that day."

"Because I had a crush on you."

"I'm sorry, Sadie," I repeat, realizing I've never apologized for that day before.

She leans her head forward, against my bare shoulder. "We're going to be a lot more sorry if people find out about this."

I lean back, forcing her to lift her head. *Fuck, I want to see her expression.* "Is that what's giving you reservations about us? That people are going to find out that we met here at the club?"

"Do *you* want people to know that?"

"I've got no intentions of telling anyone, Sadie. But what other people think of me—or us, for that matter—means very little to me in the scheme of things."

"I wish I felt the same way."

I fold my arms around her, hugging her to me. That's why she's hesitant, she fears what other people will think. And all I can think is, *That's it?* "Sadie, we can't change it. But it did give us this chance to see what happens between us, right? Maybe it wasn't such a bad decision after all."

"Do you always see the bright side of things?" I can feel her mouth twitch against my chest.

"When you've seen some of the heartbreaking and dangerous things I've seen, you tend to cling to the optimistic stuff when you can."

"Right. I'm sorry. I shouldn't be whining about this. I'm just worried. It—we, I mean—could change everything. Our families have been practically intertwined for our whole lives."

"What happens with them isn't our concern. How they react to you and me isn't our concern. My only concern is you, Sadie." My hand comes up to stroke her hair gently, hoping to ease her mind a little. "Do you trust me?" I ask as an afterthought.

There's a moment's hesitation, which makes my stomach clench in apprehension, but then Sadie nods against me. "I do."

"Then, trust me when I say that all we can do is try. I'm not promising anything to you, except that I will give it my all. Do you believe me?"

She raises her head from my chest. "I believe you."

A sense of calm washes over me. "We're really going to do this?"

Sadie's light chuckle meets my ears, making me smile. "I think we are…*Nash.*"

I push my bodyweight against her, holding her to the wall. "You know what else I think?" I ask, leaning forward and nipping at her jaw tenderly. "I think you've still got some time on the clock, *Rose.*"

"Hmm," She breathes out, tilting her head back, giving me more access to her throat. "Whatever shall we do?"

CHAPTER 11
SADIE

THERE ARE three things I know for certain now. The first is that Lydia didn't let me into the club because she remembered me, favored me, or felt sorry for me in any way. She let me in because she'd been a witness to the conversation Ashton had with his boss earlier tonight—the conversation where he'd told him that taking a chance on me was more important to him than spending his Friday nights in the belly of Club Sin. Lydia's muted amusement as she'd led me toward the Seduction Room wasn't because she pitied me, which had been my first thought as I'd pleaded with her to let me see him and followed her through the winding hallways to get there. Lydia had been smiling because she realized that I felt the same as Ashton did, that we were both willing to take a chance on each other.

The second thing I know is that I made the right choice in coming here. Not only because we'd both managed to get things off our chest that had gone unsaid for too long, but because Ashton had given me enough reassurance and hope to believe that taking this leap of faith with him wasn't a ridiculous idea, or a childish notion. We needed to give the idea of *us* a chance.

The third and final thing I know is that it's going to take a lot of time and effort for me to get over always trying to please everyone else, always trying to do the right thing, and always worrying about what others think of me and my actions. But, with Ashton's encouraging whispers and determination, I'm sure I'll get there. *We'll* get there.

And that's exactly what I'm thinking as I stand outside the back door of Club Sin, Ashton's denim jacket sprawled protectively over my shoulders to keep the chilly night air at bay. He's just ducked back inside to return his key to Christian—which he states he's never had to use, but had kept just in case of a power outage and the passcode system failing to work—and I'm smiling from ear to ear and I shift from one foot to the other in an attempt to keep warm. Never again will I wear this ridiculous dress, and if it was mine to do with as I wished, I would probably burn the damn thing.

"Sadie?"

I turn, but it's not Ashton saying my name, as the door is still closed. My eyes follow the brick wall of the building, finally landing on a tall figure in a hooded sweatshirt trudging with hesitant movements toward me. It takes me a second to place the voice, so out of context with my surroundings.

"What are you doing here?" I ask, unable to hide how mortified I am.

Gunner doesn't smile. "Funny, I was going to ask you the same question."

"I'm just…waiting…" *Damn it, damn it damn it!*

"For Ashton?" He finishes my sentence for me, each syllable labored and dripping with malice.

"Well, yes, actually." It takes everything I've got to stand tall and look at him squarely. All I really want to do is disappear under his scrutinizing gaze.

He knows.

Gunner's eyebrows rise, waiting. "And?"

"Gunner, I was going to tell you, but I wasn't even sure myself—"

The back door swings open. Ashton emerges, but his sly grin quickly morphs into a shocked expression as his mind catches up with what's playing out before him.

But he's a few beats too late. The door swings shut just as Gunner's fist slams into Ashton's jaw, knocking him hard against the brick wall.

"You fucking lied to me!" my brother screams, just as I get the words "Gunner, no!" to come out of my mouth.

Ashton's fists are clenched tightly at his sides, and miraculously, he manages to stay standing, though leaning heavily against the wall for support. He doesn't try to fight back.

I move to stand between them, but Gunner pushes me away easily, getting in another punch that connects with Ashton's shoulder when he steals a glance to make sure I'm okay.

"Gunner, stop it!" I shriek. These godforsaken heels are doing nothing to help my stance, but I dive toward my brother anyway. "Enough! If you want to blame anyone, blame me! Jesus, stop it!"

"Not only did he fucking lie to me, Sadie," Gunner barks, trying to untangle himself from my arms as I do everything I can to put myself between him and Ashton. "But he brought you *here*. Of all fucking places!"

"Ashton didn't *bring* me anywhere!" I snap. "I came here of my own accord."

That slows Gunner's struggling for a brief moment, long enough for me to get my hands fisted tightly into the shoulders of his sweatshirt.

"Why the fuck would you come—" He stops midsentence. "Sadie, what the—"

"Don't you fucking judge me," I say sharply to him, my eyes never leaving his, and my voice dripping with venom. "I'm not a kid anymore, and it's about time you realized it."

"Sin?" He screeches the word like a curse. "Shit, that's where you and those girlfriends of yours were on Friday night, weren't you?" He pauses, thinking. "Christ, that was you outside the front door earlier! I saw you! Sadie, you're better than this shit."

I don't think about it, and don't realize I've slapped him hard across the face until my hand is stinging with the impact. "I said, don't judge me, Gunner. You've got no right." I let him go, pushing him away from me in the process.

My cruel words seem to have been enough to daze him into calming down, at least enough to not throw more punches at his best friend. I'm turning to tend to Ashton, who's still leaning against the wall, his hands on his knees, breathing heavily, when a thought occurs to me. "Besides, what the hell are *you* doing here?"

Ashton's lip is bleeding, but he bats my hand gently away. His gaze is locked coldly on Gunner, who's suddenly quiet. "You didn't follow her here, did you?"

I whip around, ready to tear into my brother again for having done such a thing, but Ashton's hand is on my arm, stilling me.

"Did you come from that direction?" He points down the back alley, and when Gunner doesn't answer, I do. I catch Ashton's stare and nod at him.

"Yeah, he did. Why?" I ask.

"Because that end of the alley is blocked. This isn't a through-and-through alley, Sadie. If Gunner came from that direction, it means he came from the only exit that's down that way, and that's an exit door from Club Sin."

My eyes grow wide, and I can no longer contain myself. Shaking off Ashton's hold, I step forward and begin to bat wildly on my brother, hitting him anywhere I can make contact. "You son of a bitch!"

"Sadie! Christ, Sadie, enough, all right?" He gets a grip on my wrist and holds me there. It's then that I see the sheepishness in his eyes.

"Why is it okay for you to be in that place, and not me?" I bite out, still struggling. "That's bullshit, and you know it!"

"I'm just...I'm just—"

"Just what?" Both Ashton and I bark the words simultaneously, fed up with the conflict. I finally shrug Gunner away from me, taking a few steps back to distance myself from him, unsure if I trust myself to refrain from trying to throttle him again.

"I'm picking up my girlfriend, all right?"

I could've come up with a million things I'd expect him to say. That wasn't one of them.

"Your girl—"

As if on cue, the back door swings open again and a thin woman with her hair pulled tightly back, wrapped in a knee-length red coat, steps out into the alleyway. She sees Gunner first and beams at him. "Ready to go?"

That's when she takes in her surroundings and realizes Ashton and I are standing there, him bleeding and me looking like I'm ready to blow a gasket.

"Lydia?" Her name falls from my lips incredulously. I would lean forward and place my hands on my knees, too, to try and slow my pounding heart, if I wasn't so sure that this devil of a dress was too short to allow for it. Instead, I direct my stare toward Gunner. "Your girlfriend is Lydia?"

"What's going on here?" Lydia asks, her eyes wide, unable to comprehend what she's literally walked into the middle of.

To my surprise, Gunner reaches a hand out and guides Lydia into the crook of his arm. A gesture of protection, maybe, or comfort. "Little sister here didn't know about us, and I didn't know about them."

Them is spoken with so much disdain that it's on the tip of my tongue to lash out at him again, but Ashton reaches out for me—not quite as intimate a gesture as my brother offered Lydia, but he gets my attention, nonetheless.

"How'd you two meet?" Ashton's gaze flickers between my brother and his girlfriend, but they're both staying remarkably quiet now.

That's when I finally get it.

"You met her at Club Sin," I say. "Just like I met Ashton there, too."

"You knew him long before some stupid night at Sin, Sadie!" Gunner growls out the words, and neither Ashton nor I can hide the smirks on our faces when he realizes that he's just somehow proven that it's all okay that we're together.

Because he's right. Ashton and I have known each other our whole lives. It just took one night and a dark, coffee-and-tequila-laced mistake to bring us from the annoying and broody kids we once were, to the adults who were still searching for that something—or someone—to complete the lives we'd built for ourselves.

"You're absolutely right, my dear brother." I can't help the lighthearted tone I address him with. "So, I guess this means we can safely say that we've leveled the playing field, and our sinful secrets can stay exactly that…secrets?"

Gunner groans at my cheesy play on words, rubbing his hand down his face. But, finally, he nods. "Well played, Sadie. Well fucking played."

EPILOGUE

ASHTON

THREE MONTHS LATER...

SOME SECRETS ARE MEANT to be kept; I truly believe that.

But, some things don't have to be kept secret just because those around us might not respond well to the truth, either.

The fact that Sadie and I had a sexy rendezvous masked by darkness at Club Sin before actually realizing that our interest in each other ran deeper than just neighbors? Yeah, that's one secret that I have no issues with keeping from our families. And the fact that Gunner met Lydia while frequenting Sin, too—well, I don't know the details, and I don't want to, but I know that there's no risk to him revealing the truth to his parents anytime soon.

If the way we met ever does come to light, I guess we'll deal with it. But, for now, I don't worry about it, and I'm doing my best to make sure Sadie doesn't fret over it, either.

Besides, our parents couldn't be more ecstatic. If the Butlers and Mitchells were inseparable before, they were practically one and the same now. There'd been so many tears shed when Sadie and I sat down at one of the family dinners held at her parents' house and admitted we'd been seeing each other behind their backs, I honestly wondered if someone was going to drown in the wake of it.

Every one of those tears was shed with happiness, though. Anna Mitchell bawled like a baby, then broke out the champagne, and my mother hugged us both so tightly that I thought Sadie might break under the force of it. Then, Mom had thanked us—actually *thanked* us—for getting together... like we'd somehow done it for the sake of their friendship with the Mitchells or something. It was a little misguided, but whatever works. No one got angry, and no one asked if we'd met each other at a sex club, so all things considered, I'd say it went over as well as it could.

Gunner and Lydia announced their impending engagement about a month later. It turns out they'd been seeing each other for close to seven months, a lot longer than anyone realized. I figure I probably should've been miffed that he didn't feel he could tell me he was seeing someone, but seeing as I lied to his face about anything going on between me and Sadie, and never have formally admitted to him that I actually worked at Sin—and I know he knows; there's no way Lydia wouldn't tell him—I'm going to call it even and make a mental note never to lie to the man again.

Anyway, with an engagement party to plan, and then a wedding, I should probably thank Gunner and Lydia for getting our parents off Sadie and I's backs. Both Anna and my mom adore Lydia, so they've got their claws into her, undoubtedly driving her insane with fabric swatches, cake samples, and wine choices, even if it's only Anna's son getting married to the poor girl.

Good luck to Lydia and Gunner with that. They're going to need it.

But, that's left Sadie and me more time to figure each other out.

Alone.

Knowing each other our whole lives, and relearning who we are more intimately as adults…it's different. Every day, there are things she says or does that catch my attention, tidbits of information I never knew, or true colors that shine through. Things she's hidden from the world since she was a little girl.

Things that make me fall harder for her every single day.

Things I think about often, even when I don't realize it.

"Why are you smiling?"

Sadie's voice pulls me from my thoughts, and I laugh when I see her, her head turned awkwardly to the side as she stares at me, perplexed.

We're sprawled out together on the couch, her back pressed solidly against my chest and my leg draped over her shins, holding her against me. One of the *Fast & Furious* movies plays on the TV, but neither of us is really paying much attention to it.

"I guess I'm just thinking," I tell her, nuzzling my face into her hair. The vanilla scent of her shampoo ignites a spark of desire within me.

"I knew you couldn't possibly be paying attention when they just drove that car off the bridge and you didn't even bother to tell me how impossible that is." She chuckles, and the infectious sound has me pulling her nearer to me, desperate to be as close as I can get.

"It's hard to focus on car chases when I've got your sexy little body tucked up against me." I rock my hips forward, and she lets out a little squeal. The woman knows exactly what I'm talking about.

"Tell me what you're thinking about, and maybe it'll help me get up to speed."

She shifts her weight, turning to face me, and I slide an

arm around her back, pulling her up onto me. "Oh, you've got it all wrong, Sadie. No speed. I'll take my time." I kiss her lips tenderly. "Pain…" Then her jaw. "…stakingly…" Then her neck. "…slow. You'll be begging me for more, I guarantee it."

Her eyes flutter in response to my lips on her neck. It's one of the places I know makes her weak with desire instantly.

"Yeah?" she breathes. "Don't you have to go into the fire-hall tonight?"

Night shift. *Shit.*

"Damn it, yes. And you have that wine tasting thing with Lydia and your mom." All it takes is one taste or touch from Sadie, and I tend to forget everything else around us. Judging by the smirk tugging at the corner of her lips, I'd say she finds that fact a bit amusing.

"So, you'll go to work, I'll go to the wine tasting and get half-lit, and we'll meet back here to reconvene."

I scoff dramatically. "Well, when you put it like that, it all just sounds so damn romantic."

Sadie laughs, rolling her eyes. "I'm sorry…you know I still adore you."

"Adore?" I arch a brow high on my forehead. "I think you meant love. You still love me."

"Maybe I do," she teases. "Maybe I love you a heck of a lot. What've you got to say about that?"

We've never formally said those three little words to each other, not yet. But, I must admit, that sounds pretty much like the real thing to me.

"I think I would have to say that I love you, too."

"Yeah?" She nuzzles into me, pressing her forehead to mine. "I think you should prove it."

"Hmm. Got something in mind, doll?"

I'm still grinning as she pulls away from me and stretches her arm out, grabbing her cellphone from the table. "It's about five o'clock," she says with a grin. "We've got about an hour."

"An hour," I repeat, sliding my hands over her back, tucking my fingers into her back pockets. "The magic number of minutes. How can we possibly fill an entire hour?"

"Start the clock, *Nash*, and tell me what you want." She giggles, her eyebrows waggling mischievously.

It's become a game, recreating our night at Club Sin, coming up with all the ways that one-hour interval could've gone. It's intriguing, and sexy as hell.

I swing my legs off the couch, taking Sadie with me as I stand, much to her amusement. "I'm pretty sure it's your turn to call the shots, *Rose*, if my memory serves me right."

Her legs are wrapped around my hips as I carry her toward the bedroom. "Close the blinds and turn off the lights," she instructs, already breathless. "I've heard being robbed of your sense of sight can really heighten your other senses."

"Smart man, whoever told you that."

"We'll see if you still believe that when I'm done with you."

"You've only got an hour, doll."

"And I told you, start the clock. I want to show you how much I love you."

This. This, right here, is what I've been missing. Being in love, being loved, and loving someone else. I took a winding, rocky path to find it, but I *did* find it. Find *her*.

This is what I'm made for. Loving Sadie Mitchell. It just took me a lifetime to figure it out.

And a little sin.

ABOUT THE AUTHOR

Cass Kincaid writes steamy romance stories, creates HEAs, and loves every damn minute of it. She LOVES love, and she's a hopeless romantic. Oh, and she has a thing for sexy, sarcastic fictional boyfriends, but don't we all?

ABOUT THE PUBLISHER

EverLust Books is an imprint of Harbor Lane Books, LLC. We are a US-based independent digital publisher of steamy contemporary romance to erotic fiction.

Connect with EverLust Books on our website www.everlustbooks.com and TikTok, Instagram, and Twitter @everlustbooks.